Over The Top

A "Dying to Be Fit" Novel

Nancy Klotz

OverTheTop is a work of fiction. Names, characters, locations, and events are either products of the author's imagination or are used fictitiously. Any resemblance to actual persons, living or dead, locales, or events are entirely coincidental.

Published in the United States of America by Nancy Klotz.

Cover Design by DiamondD.Net

Copyright © 2014 Nancy Klotz

All rights reserved.

ISBN: 978-06922008830

DEDICATION

To Bud and his retirement

ACKNOWLEDGEMENTS

The author relied on the help of several people in the writing of this book. Special thanks to Leslie Urbaniak. Many thanks also to Nikki Young, Marie Dickinson, Duncan Dickinson, Cari Hammar, Bud Klotz, Deb Kiel, and Carol Todd.

ONE

DID I MAKE the right decision? Should I have made a different choice? Did I take the best option? I question myself a lot. Self-doubt is my biggest enemy, or so I thought. My current mantra is 'living life with confidence and ease' to help counter my anxiety.

I am Claudia Monroe, and I own OverTheTop Gym. Buying the gym was a new and risky venture for me, and I am always marketing and trying to keep the business going. I bought OverTheTop from a company that was going under and have a lot of competition in the fitness industry. There are newer, big, glass and chrome, and glitzy gyms, like Life Magic, and smaller gyms that have been here forever, like PowerUp, a local neighborhood gym. I keep thinking like a scramble, always moving around trying to brand my gym as something special so that we attract more members. We have to market the reason why our place is different from the others and how our services are better than the rest.

What people really want is a place to call home, a place where they feel comfortable and can socialize with their peers. The location of the gym is great! We are within walking distance from downtown MidTown, but far enough a way so that we have our own parking. The location is all very convenient for us as employees and for our members. Do I have what it takes to keep the gym open, running, and profitable? Should I have taken the risk to begin with?

Standing at the front counter, I felt a gusty breeze blow into the gym as the front door opened. In the Midwest, late September and October temperatures can range from the thirties to the nineties just depending on the year. Charlene, my assistant, arrived with her morning box of chocolate covered donuts. I stood at the front counter greeting clients as they arrived for their personal training sessions. The wind and a few more leaves blew in the large glass door again as Mick Ballard entered to train with Susan, one of our personal trainers. I sent him to the back of the building where the lockers are so he could change his clothes and get ready for his work out.

The front counter is like the main gathering place at the gym. It's similar to when you go to a party and everyone hangs out in the kitchen, even when there's lots of space somewhere else in the house. The gold granite counter top is about 12 feet long, chest height, with black and rust colored accents. Members and employees all come in the front door and pass the counter. We exchange membership cards for locker keys as people come and go.

Charlene has a fetish for chocolate covered anything in the mornings. She keeps her stash hidden until no one is around to see her eat. She actually has a cubbyhole behind the counter to hide her food until she feels safe bringing it out.

"Uh oh," said Charlene. "Here comes the Tiger Lady."

"You better hide that box of donuts before we get a lecture," I said. "Although I am sure she can smell a donut from a hundred yards away."

The Tiger Lady is one of our group fitness instructors who has the willpower and principles of a great beast, hence the nickname behind her back – Tiger Lady. Her lean and muscular build shows off as she tells her class why they are more 'rounded' than she is, why their bodies are soft and hers is firm. She knows they would eat a muffin when she would choose an apple. Charlene and I are certain a chocolate covered donut of any kind has ever passed through her lips. The members love her, her classes fill regularly, and she proudly announces to her following how many people attend her classes each day. They wish they looked like her, compact and buff.

I am in my late forties, tall and fairly fit. I have blue eyes and blond hair that is usually pulled back in a ponytail like most of the other exercise instructors.

Don't confuse me with a dumb blond, as my intelligence and common sense usually save the day for me even with the most challenging of people. I normally wear spandex or sweats with an athletic wicking top. My bright, positive smile shines out for most people; usually my attitude is genuine, but also necessary for great customer service. I like my nails polished with matching colors on my hands and feet! I am fairly strong and work out most days of the week, alternating between, cardio, strength, mind/body, and flexibility.

My intention is to grow a thriving fitness business because I am passionate about fitness and also want to create employment for myself! The business side of the gym is not always my favorite part of the job.

Charlene will talk to anybody. I keep her working where she is needed the most, often the front counter. She is one of those people who always seems to be eating something, but never seems to gain weight. Don't we all wish we had her metabolism? Perky is a good word to describe her. She is one of those short and thin people that surprise you with their big presence. Even her black hair is all spikey on top. She's full of energy and comes across as positive and happy. She wears spandex too, but more as a fashion statement than for working out. I'm not sure she actually works out, but no one else gets that impression. Charlene projects fitness.

OverTheTop

"Good morning," Tiger Lady said. Her real name is Becca Bloom and she has been in this business longer than I have. "Seems like winter came earlier than we expected, even though fall only officially started a little more than a week ago."

"You are right. It is cold!" I replied. "Have a great class."

"I always do," she said as she breezed past us, headed for the aerobic studio. Becca is one of those instructors where half the class doesn't show up if they know she has a sub and will not be teaching that day.

"Can't wait to see what your numbers are today!" Charlene called after her.

Charlene brought out the donuts and started eating. I told her not to get them near me or I would gain weight just smelling them!

"How can you say no to donuts day after day?" she asked.

"My problems are multi-fold, Charlene. I love chocolate and I snack when I'm hungry or stressed, so by the end of the day when my resolve is down, I will binge on chocolate or a snack whether I have eaten a donut in the morning or not. That's overeating twice in one day. I will have double ruined my points."

"Geez. Hearing how much you think things through hurts my brain. Sugar, fat, and chocolate all fried up and put together in a donut are the best," Charlene said.

Our personal training business is picking up. We currently have over 200 clients that train privately or in small groups. Our overall membership runs about 1,500. All of our staff, instructors and trainers, are nationally certified and provide great customer service with customized training programs for our clients.

Bob, one of our trainers, came through the front door and said, "You ought to move that counter so it isn't right in line to catch cold air from the door."

He looked at the donuts.

"Good way to advertise fitness, Charlene. Can I have one?" Charlene looked around to make sure no one could see and handed him a donut.

"Great idea about the front counter," I replied. "I'll think on it. Your new client is coming in at ten. She filled out her health and activity history forms. Why don't you take her into one of the multi-purpose training rooms so everything will be available for her depending on what you guys decide her goals and interests are? Her name is Beth McMan."

Each multi-purpose training room contained a wide variety of equipment such as a bench, ball, Bosu, free weights, tubing, body bars, and a cardio machine like a treadmill or elliptical trainer. The rooms were separated with a partitioned wall to give clients the feeling of privacy.

Sometimes a person will choose personal training for the sole purpose of not wanting to workout in front of other people. Self-consciousness is a real issue for many people. The reason they are self-conscious may be real or not real. Some clients feel that way because of size, shape, weight, ability level, fitness level, experience, coordination, self importance, and loneliness. Some don't want to take their socks off for Pilates or yoga! With practice and training, most of these obstacles go away.

"Thanks. I'll take care of her," Bob said. "Here's one for you. How do snails breath?"

"Dunno."

"Through their feet."

"Huh," I said.

He went back to the multi-purpose room.

Bob was our trivia nut and asked the most random questions at the most random times. I couldn't quite figure out who had time to look up all the quirky little facts that he asked. Who even cared? He was part of our team, so we tolerated the trivia. And truthfully, every once in a while, he came up with some really interesting tidbit of information.

I checked an item off on my to-do list. "Another one down."

"Nuh uh," Charlene said. "I only ate the two donuts you saw me eat."

"Charlene. I wasn't counting the number of donuts you are eating! I'm just scratching things off my 'to do' list for the day."

Later that morning one of my clients, Sam Good, came in for training. He was into heavy lifting and increasing strength. We went back to a multi-purpose room to work legs with squats and lunges. Sam is a fine specimen of a man. He's pleasant to look at when he's lifting and any other time. He's blond and stands about six feet tall. He has spectacular muscle definition in most areas of his body, of what I can see that is.

After training, as Sam was leaving, Charlene leaned towards me and said, "Now, you tell me about that Hunk of a Man."

"Charlene, that hunk of man's name is Sam. You know that trainer/client information is confidential. No way I'm telling."

"There is no way anything is confidential about that man. He is out there for the public to admire," said Charlene.

Sam is in his thirties, tall, nice looking, and built like a brick house. His blond hair and tan makes him look healthy and relaxed. He comes in almost every day for cardio and lifting, taking two days a week to train. Charlene perks up and then drools every time she sees him. She really has drooling issues when he wears spandex.

The truth be known, Sam and I share enough time and conversation together to be considered friends. I know men and women are capable of friendship. Many times, in life, I have noticed that if there is an attraction, men and women friends don't always stop at friendship, even when circumstances like marriage are in the way. He's a good guy, and we tease each other and talk about life events and feelings. I'm not sure having a more meaningful relationship would work with us.

"I want a man like that. And he's single too. You're an old married woman so you just don't notice," said Charlene.

"Oh, I notice, I just don't try the goods, but I bet his goods are just fine," I replied.

After we closed for the day, I went to see my Internet marketing guru. He lives on the other side of town and works in his home. Joe Ellis is a geek. Why all computer geeks are stereotyped to look similar is no mystery to me. Joe was good, real good, at anything technology related. He wore thick glasses, had a bit of grease in his black hair, and was bent over his computer when I arrived.

"I got your marketing materials all set up and linked from the website to the blog to Facebook and back again. It's all optimized to come up on the first page of hits when someone searches for a local fitness center."

Some of the common search tags are fitness, gym, MidTown, health, exercise, and personal training. The marketing campaign Joe set up on the Internet was just what I wanted.

Well, I couldn't ask for more, could I? I needed to keep the business in the limelight, and Joe does excellent work. He is one of MidTown's best kept secrets. He understands all those technical things that people don't even know enough to ask questions about. He can fix glitches and make changes to our media seamlessly. We are very thankful to have Joe on our side.

My mind relaxed now that I was on my way home for the night.

TWO

THE NEXT MORNING when I arrived at the gym in my standard spandex pants, wicking top, and ponytail, a crowd of seven people had gathered around the front counter to gossip. Evidently there was a local news story about one of our clients, Mick Ballard, being involved in a huge embezzlement scheme. His real estate company, The Golden Door, was producing two different rental agreements for all the rental property he was accountable for. The first lease agreement went to the renter at a particular rental rate per month, say $500. The second lease agreement went to the corporations that owned the apartments and hired Mick's company to handle their rentals, Real Estate Ventures. This agreement had a lower rental rate recorded, like $450. The difference in rates, in this example $50 per unit, was nowhere to be found. Of course, Mick claimed innocence, with 'prove it was me' as a defense. He was still out and about, but I wondered how his reputation would fare with all the bad publicity he was getting.

Mick is tall and good-looking in a distinguished way. He's in his fifties and usually wears suits and ties. He comes across as confident and knowledgeable, like somebody you would want on your side in a controversy. His gray hair was part of his persona, like a trademark, adding the distinguished part to his list of characteristics. He started The Golden Door probably 20 years ago, and the company had grown to the point where it managed at least half of the rental properties in town. Mick personal trained with Susan since before I took ownership of OverTheTop.

Tiger Lady came through the front door and looked at the sign up sheet for her cycle class. She smiled smugly when she noted all the bikes were taken. Her class was full again. She subconsciously, or not, flexed her biceps as she walked into the cycle room. She was wearing black and red Specialized cycle gear from head to toe. You would think she was riding in a race sponsored by Specialized.

"Let's go ask Susan what she knows about Mick," said Charlene as she popped a chocolate covered donut into her mouth. "He was just in here training with her yesterday."

We walked towards the multi-purpose rooms to find her. Susan is tall and thin, like me, with a cute face and long straight hair. She is one of our star trainers, and Mick trains with her twice a week. She listens well to clients and has a good feel for what motivates and interests people. She is very meticulous about keeping client records up to date and journals each of her sessions.

"He seemed calm and okay to me yesterday," she said. "But that's about all I can say. He worked hard."

"I know. I know. All that confidentiality stuff again," said Charlene.

"Charlene, do you have any donuts left today?" asked Susan.

"I sure do. I saved two, one for you and one for me."

"How about jogging on the Riverwalk later?" Susan asked as she ate her donut.

"Nah, I'll take a pass. We could meet for nachos later tonight though," said Charlene.

The Riverwalk is a path that runs through town along the MidTown River. People walk, jog, and feed the ducks on the Riverwalk. Bicycling is not permitted until the path heads out of the downtown area. In the downtown area many storefronts face the Riverwalk providing free advertising and potential revenue for the stores.

"Hey," Bob said walking into the room while we were talking to Susan. "How fast can a turkey run?"

We all rolled our eyeballs.

"Dunno."

"Twenty miles per hour," Bob answered.

"Huh," I said.

I know he's cute and interesting, but do I really care about how fast turkeys run? And where in my brain would I have room to store information like that? I have enough on my mind just trying to keep the business running.

We all disbursed and went about our schedules, including manning the front desk, training, working membership, and marketing. Before I knew it, lunch had passed. I walked to the local sandwich shop and bought a sandwich to go. Chicken salad sat on top of two English muffins covered with melted cheese. The meal came with fries and a little side salad. Yum.

Later that day, with our new marketing campaign going, our phone was ringing more than usual. Charlene was busy answering the calls and filing client folders. A young lady, small and attractive with a full head of red hair, came to the front desk and said she had an appointment with Susan. Since Susan hadn't come to greet her client, I went to the training rooms to find her. She was no where to be found; I paged her. After waiting for a few minutes, I apologized to the new client, Helen, and completed her initial consultation myself. We set up a time for her first training session before she left.

"What happened to Susan? She was just here!" asked Charlene.

"I don't know...but it is very unlike her to miss an appointment. She may have just lost a client to me!"

"Well, I know Joe is definitely worth the marketing money, because business and appointments are picking up already! Susan won't get too far behind you in number of clients," said Charlene.

As we were getting ready to leave for the day, Charlene asked me if I wanted to go out for nachos.

"No thanks," I said. "I'm going home to my own hunk of a man."

We lived in a typical suburban neighborhood on a cul de sac where none of the neighbors speak to one another. We have a nice sized house with four bedrooms, an office, and a finished basement. Our front yard was small enough to make us close to the neighbors, but our backyard was great! Surrounded by a six-foot fence, the yard extends to a half an acre. We can sit in the backyard and see all sorts of nature, like, birds, squirrels, and dragonflies. A set of owls live nearby. At least two owls talk to each other loud enough for us to hear. Matt, our dog, likes to run and play in the yard.

There are a couple of different kinds of neighborhoods. One is where the neighbors meet regularly and socialize. They make up any reason to have a party. And then there's ours. No one speaks to each other even if we are all out working in our front yards at the same time. Sometimes if I see one neighbor in particular, I wait until she is gone before I go out. Avoiding contact with your neighbors can be a little uncomfortable and inconvenient at times.

Our dog, Matt, is my best buddy. He waits faithfully at home for me each night hoping to take a walk through the neighborhood. His unconditional love for me is something many people would envy. Who can really say they have unconditional love?

Max is my hunk of a man, and he had dinner waiting. What a guy! We were having grilled fish and cubed butternut squash. As we ate dinner, we talked about our days in general. Max is slightly younger than me, slightly taller than me, and just started shaving his head.

We were married several years ago, both of us surviving divorces and having children in tow. Other than a few angry moments now and then, we appreciate each other's company. We also enjoy a robust sex life, and tonight was no exception. We usually go upstairs to our bedroom and fool around. I think many couples have their own little sayings and subtle hints referring to their sex lives. Ours is "Do you want to go upstairs?" Not terribly original, but very effective. Max travels regularly for his work, so when he's home, we usually take advantage of the time together.

THREE

CHARLENE CALLED MY cell phone before I got out of bed in the morning. "I don't know where Susan is. I left messages at her home and on her cell and she never got back to me. We were going to have nachos last night."

I told Charlene that Susan might have met someone, gotten sick, visited family, or lost her phone. I felt sure we would see her or hear from her when we got to work.

Bob was opening the gym that day, and surprisingly, Susan wasn't there when we arrived. No one received any voicemails from her on their cells or on the main business line at the gym. Charlene wanted me to go to her condo to check up on her and make sure everything was okay.

"We haven't seen her for 24 hours," she said.

"How would I even get in?" I asked.

"I know she keeps a spare key in her locker here, and of course I have the keys to the lockers," Charlene said.

"She may just have a life, Charlene. Although, it's unusual for her not to call in if she is running late. I'll check the schedule to see what time she has clients today," I said. Then I assigned Bob to train Susan's client that was already scheduled for early morning.

Reluctantly, I headed over to Susan's condo to check on her. Charlene stayed at the front counter to answer calls and check members in. I walked over on the sidewalk because she lived only a few blocks away from work. The air had warmed up a little, and maple trees, still green from the summer, lined each side of the street. A few of the leaves were starting to change color.

Susan's condo was in Midwest Winds, the third building in a group of eight condo buildings - #3C. She recently had Charlene and I over for a girls' wine night out. I banged the decorative brass knocker on her metal door and called her name. Nothing. I opened the door with her key and knocked and called out again. Nothing. Going inside her place felt strange, but I agreed that we needed to make sure she was okay. The modern furnishings in the living room all matched. The walls were painted a neutral light gray; the trim and baseboards were painted white. I like white trim. It reminds me of the south.

OverTheTop

There was a bookshelf covered with many fitness reference books and training manuals, some easy reading books, and trade magazines. I called out again as I walked to the bedroom. This felt very eerie, like being in an empty school building alone after dark. The bedroom had a queen size bed, a dresser, and a nightstand with a cute lamp on top. The bottom shelf of the nightstand held some journals and what looked like a diary. Other than that, the room had a few family pictures and a photograph on the wall.

I saw a blinking light on the answering machine and assumed it was Charlene's message. I checked out the bathroom and saw her makeup there, along with a toothbrush. But who knows? Maybe she has a travel bag of cosmetics. Next I went into the kitchen. Nothing of interest there. It didn't look like she had eaten or made a meal recently. Oh well, what did this adventure tell us? Not much, other than Susan did not show up for work.

As I walked back in the gym, Charlene was eating a chocolate éclair, and Bob handed me the phone saying it was Max.

Moving away from listening ears, I said, "Hey, baby. No sorry. I can't go to lunch today. I am a guest speaker at that Lady's Club today. You know, gotta promote the business."

"Okay baby. Bye," I hung up.

I told Charlene and Bob that I found nothing unusual at Susan's, but described the empty feeling and silence that permeated the condo.

The Lady's Club luncheon was at the local country club. The members were mostly middle aged and promoted community service, as well as self-development. I donated a personal training session for their upcoming silent auction charity event.

The clubhouse and golf course were a couple of miles away from downtown. The building itself looked like a large Tudor home. Inside, the building was divided into a restaurant, pro shop, and locker rooms. There was a large open banquet room, but we had lunch in the restaurant.

At the luncheon, I stood at a podium in the front of the room and discussed planning ahead to bring exercise inside for the winter. Some options were joining the gym, investing in a cardio machine, using exercise videos, and getting some weights, a ball, and tubing. Another choice was to hire a trainer to help you design a program that you could follow for the winter.

When I was through, a lady in a bright animal print jacket raised her hand to ask a question. She said, "I took one of your classes and you did ballistic stretching. Why?" I stared at her blankly because I had no idea what she was talking about. She got up and started pulsing pliés beside her table, looking a little crazy. I wasn't going to argue with her, but explained the difference between dynamic and static stretching, and how an exercise and a stretch are not necessarily the same thing. I also talked about changing the tempo and rhythm in an exercise to vary the way the muscle works. She didn't react well, so I thanked her for her comments and asked if there were any other questions.

Usually I respond with a "Good question!" People seem to feel better for asking. Not this time, with this woman. There is definitely a cast of characters in this world who think they know a lot more than they do. Or just think they are right. Or need to be right.

Before we left the gym that evening, Charlene insisted on calling the police to report Susan as missing. She told the officer that Susan did not come to work that day. The officer informed her that a person had to be missing 48 hours before the police got involved. He said that 70,000 people a year go missing from the Chicagoland area alone. After the call, we figured out that 70,000 people a year meant about 192 people a day went missing.

"You can go by her condo on your way home for peace of mind, Charlene," I said. She took the key and left.

When I got home, Max had grilled cheese and tomato soup waiting. He told me that our 'mean neighbor,' Genna, caught him on his way in to the house to complain about some branches on our tree that hung over her property line. That woman, really? The only time she spoke to us was to complain about one thing or another. I can't understand how a person can be angry so much of the time. I assumed she wasn't born that way, so I wondered what happened in her life to make her perpetually mad. A stern expression was permanently embedded on her face. She was slim, middle height, and had short brown hair. I think she worked out somewhere else because occasionally I saw her in workout clothes carrying a gym bag and sporting a ball cap. At OverTheTop, we don't need members like her. I'm sure we have a few, but don't want anymore.

    Max and I talked about Susan's disappearance as we walked Matt around the block that night. We both agreed that something was up, her professionalism and personality would not allow her to just check out of her responsibilities, although the answer could go several ways like she met someone, had an emergency, or was in trouble. There could be a wide variety of reasons. We didn't have the answer, but hoped for the best and knew that the issue would unfold.

FOUR

WRITING ARTICLES FOR community newspapers is another way to market a company. The next morning I stayed at home on my computer writing until I had two solid articles to submit. One article was about exercising outside in the fall. I talked about our town's limestone trails through the county's forest preserves. Hey, you can walk, jog, ride your bike, or take your dog to any of those places. I also talked about the outdoor yoga class that OverTheTop would be having before the weather was too cold using outdoor patio heaters. The other article was about circumstances where you might be better off with a personal trainer, like figuring out how to get started on a workout routine or exercising with an injury.

At my age, resigning from my stable position as a teacher in a neighboring school district was a big risk.

Max and I discussed having our own business and we agreed that I should give the gym everything I had to make it a success. Fitness is a passion for both of us.

Max has a very solid personality, and generally takes life calmly and matter of factly. However, without my steady income from teaching, and with the fluctuating sales and expenses from owning a new business, Max decided that maybe we had been too hasty in our decision making. Too late. Now that I knew this venture made him nervous, some of the fun was gone for me, and in place I had additional pressure to perform. I couldn't figure out how someone could turn around on an agreement so quickly. He still said he supported me, but I didn't feel like I could go to him with many of the challenges of the business for fear of making him too anxious. I ended up getting levels of support from my network of friends and co-workers that I wished I could get from him.

Max was headed out of town again tomorrow to Indiana to work on a plant that his company was installing from scratch, floor to ceiling. He owned his company with a partner, and represented the engineering side, getting patents for many of his ideas. He ended up out in the field a lot, changing his ideas into reality.

As I drove to work, I thought about my gratitude list. I came up with a list of things to be grateful for in life that fits on a regular typed sheet of paper in three columns. Then on the printed paper I have written more words in the margins and in between columns. My car, an old Toyota 4Runner, is near the top of the list and has never let me down. The four-wheel drive gets me wherever I need to go in any weather. Reliability is important in the Midwest. My two kids, Marissa and Steve, want my car for the winter. It's the bomb!

Charlene was tasting homemade cream puffs from the local bakery when I got to the gym. She thought they were more than excellent with real custard in the middle and thick chocolate frosting on the outside. I declined. Call me crazy. Subconsciously, I knew my day of overindulgence would be coming.

In slow, down times, between clients and members, we decided to speculate on what could have happened to Susan. We wrote a list of some of her favorite places: the coffee shop, the Riverwalk, the Mac store, the fitness accessory store.

Later, I walked down the street to get coffee and check on Susan. The coffee shop is on a corner lot with windows on two sides of the building that had views of the Riverwalk. Camille, the barista, knows many customers who frequent the coffee shop on a regular basis. She is slightly short and stout with natural colored pink cheeks. I asked her if she had seen Susan.

"I saw her – let's see – that would be two days ago before lunch. She got a coffee and – I remember her recognizing someone on her way out. A man, tall, graying hair. I didn't pay much attention." I told her thanks and took the coffee back to the gym.

Sam Good was coming in for training causing Charlene to be perky and drooling. I took him back to the multi-purpose room closest to the free weight section and the weight machines. He started working his chest with the cables. His chest is a sight to see. The scenery is amazing. Luckily, we have an easy, casual rapport.

"Claudia, you are looking good these days," Sam said. I could feel his eyes on me as I thanked him. He set up for a bench press while I spotted him. I could feel the heat coming from his body.

"Would you be interested in meeting outside the gym?" he asked.

"What did you have in mind?" I asked. I wasn't very sure where this was going, but I hoped I was wrong. Sam was a very tempting man, but I saw red, first because I was married, and second, you don't dally with your clients. Well, in real life you aren't supposed to dally if you stay professional. Besides, I know we liked each other as friends and didn't know where anything more would lead.

"We could take our friendship beyond what we have from personal training," Sam suggested.

"I'm thinking not," I said. "But thank you for the compliment. It's just too sketchy to try and have a male/female relationship. We have a pretty good one the way it is." Sam and I usually talk openly about issues in life.

He smiled slightly.

"Can't blame me for trying."

Often clients and trainers develop relationships that are based on trust and clients share personal feelings and information with their trainers. The outcome can border on therapy or best friends forever. Sometimes that professional relationship along with being physically close to each other can cause two people to cross a line and start whatever kind of affair they have in mind.

Bob walked close to where we were working because he was training one of Susan's clients, and the moment with Sam passed.

After Sam's training session was over, I manned the front counter while Charlene went to check out the fitness accessory store and the Mac store to see if anyone remembered seeing Susan in the last day or two. She took a copy of Susan's professional mug shot with her, looking glum when she returned.

"Nothing," she said. "Well, it's been 48 hours, I'm calling the police again."

An hour later Detective Andrews came to the gym and took as much information as we had about the timeline before and after Susan had last been seen. He said he would investigate, but didn't appear too worried. His manner was slow and laid back. His brown hair was a little shaggy and he wore a coat similar to a trench coat. With his average height and looks, he kind of blended into the scenery. We didn't get our hopes up.

"If they don't have any information by tomorrow morning, let's jog down the Riverwalk to see what we can see," I said.

Charlene said, "How 'bout we walk down the Riverwalk – get it? River – walk."

"Sure, that way you can eat your donuts and drink your coffee as we go," I said.

I wasn't sure what we were looking for, but knew that Susan used the trails a lot. I was worried that no one was taking her absence seriously enough. Disappearing was out of character for her.

The Riverwalk is a beautiful place to have in the community. The trail is made of uniform interlocking bricks making a pathway that is several miles long. It runs along the river and then into the woods.

We have Bodywalk classes that leave the gym and powerwalk for three miles on the Riverwalk. The class is very popular on pretty days with good weather. Although we didn't invent walking, members still love going outside together to exercise. Just as a marketing afterthought, we also have cycling classes outside and a running club.

"I'll ask Bob if he can open up tomorrow morning to give us time to walk down the Riverwalk," I said.

Bob is quite a ladies' man. He is dark with unruly hair, medium height, and is very well defined. He can be a real charmer, too. Rumor has it that he has done 'it' in the stairwell at the gym. I smile every time I go up the stairwell in the back, but hope to heaven 'it' wasn't with a client! I checked upstairs to make sure the exercise room was empty and equipment was put away then I left to drive home.

Later that night, Max and I talked about all the avenues I was taking to keep the business going in the right direction. Up. In the black.

We also talked about kid issues. Between the two of us we had four adult children ranging in age from 20 to 26. My two children, Steve and Marissa, lived in apartments in the area. Marissa is a wiz at technology type stuff. Steve is a terrific sales person who enjoys exercise and being outside. Max has a son, Clark, who lives in Santa Cruz, California. He surfs and works in the surfing business for a living. He amuses us when he describes the nature of a wave and how you need to be at just the right spot at just the right time to ride the wave. Max's daughter, Emily, lives in Texas working as a financial counselor to college students. Max hates the heat down there. Mostly the kids all want money.

Max and I seldom agree on how to raise children. We've taken to not talking about them too much. Having a blended family is not an easy road to travel. I truly feel empathy for any parents with blended families. I also feel for the kids because very often they end up being the losers in a battle between adults.

Our conversation turned to Susan being reported as a missing person. I told him that Detective Andrews didn't seem like a fireball of enthusiasm and that Charlene and I were checking out places that

Susan frequented. He was concerned, but glad that her disappearance was officially police business. Sometimes I think his calmness comes from not thinking too deeply about situations that don't involve him directly.

Thankfully Max and I enjoy sex with each other because sometimes the sex can help us forget or let go of differences in opinion. Being together is something we have in common. With four now adult children and a new small business, we often have to agree to disagree.

FIVE

THE COOL, FALL morning was brisk with sunny skies. Charlene, with her donut and coffee, met me at the start of the Riverwalk west of Main Street where we walked our way west down by the river and into the woods. We followed the path through downtown along the MidTown River. We saw nothing out of the ordinary. What were we expecting anyway?

Retracing our steps, we crossed Main Street and Second Street to reach the other side. There weren't as many people enjoying this side of the trail. When we were near the end of the pavers where the concrete bike trail joins the path, we saw a swatch of red material in the bushes closest to the river. We moved off the side of the trail, walked through the bushes and trees to the river's edge.

"Uh Blafffff." Charlene threw up into the brush. I scrambled back as fast as I could, breathing heavily, and dialed 911 on my cell. We had stumbled on the body of Susan.

Her body was stiff, bloated, swollen, and bluish. Her upper body was in the water at the edge of the river with her legs and hips stretched towards the water settling against some rocks on the side. Because of the way she was sprawled out, the water, fish or animals, and nature had taken a toll on her body.

Charlene and I huddled together on the path, crying and waiting for the police. Even though Susan's body was off the beaten path, behind bushes and trees, we didn't know why someone wouldn't have spotted her already. The sight and feel of her death was just so shocking, surreal, dead.

I felt curious looking at a dead body. At funerals, sometimes the deceased looks like it could inhale and start breathing, but not Susan's body. My insides went cold and hard, unbelieving. I had to take slow deep yoga breaths to try to calm down. The only other dead body I've seen besides at funerals was when I went to pick up Max's dad for breakfast, and he had died while sitting in a chair watching a ball game.

We stood back as the police secured the crime scene. Detective Andrews listened to our story, took our statements, and told us he would follow up with us at the gym later today.

OverTheTop

As we walked towards the gym Charlene asked, "Well, what did we think we would find by walking down the Riverwalk? That Susan had been strolling up and down for three days?"

"No one else was looking for her that we could tell. We had to do something."

When we opened the door, Bob said, "Mick Ballard came by to train with Susan, but did not want to stay and train with me." Bob must have noticed our faces because he asked, "What is wrong?"

Tiger Lady walked in and stopped in her tracks when she saw our expressions and state of disrepair. "Don't tell me my class is cancelled. What could possibly be the matter?"

Tears spilled out of Charlene's eyes as I told them Susan was dead.

Shock is an interesting feeling and is hard to describe. Shock is upsetting, surprising, and leaves your body feeling like it can't function effectively. Surroundings seem surreal. Telling them the most basic of the details was challenging.

Detective Andrews arrived at the building and closed the gym to anyone entering or leaving until they were interviewed. His crew asked the staff and members questions about when they had last seen Susan and what their relationship to her was.

He wanted the list of members of OverTheTop Gym. I didn't know what to do. I watch TV and see people say, "Not without a search warrant." I know client files are confidential, but I couldn't justify keeping names confidential in light of the circumstances. However, I did not really want the cops talking to all the members and telling them an employee was murdered. I wondered why I thought the word - murdered - and not accidental. I'm sure the members would all find out, but did the cops really need to bring it to their attention? Several cops on the police investigation team questioned the people currently at the gym.

The medical examiner estimated that the time of death was over 48 hours ago. We saw her last about 10 am three days ago when we asked her about Mick.

Not wanting to sound indifferent because I'm not. I'm devastated. But I wondered how a murder would affect business at the gym and how closing the gym for the morning hours would sit with the members. I know Tiger Lady wasn't happy.

The house was empty when I walked in that night. I love to be alone, although being alone is rare. I took out leftover chicken noodle soup and butternut squash cubes and heated them up in the microwave. Matt was happy to be by my side.

I felt tired and drained of energy when Max called to say he was sorry to be out of town when something tragic like this happened. He wanted to know if he should come home, and I told him there really wasn't anything he could do. I described what shock felt like to me, but wasn't sure he understood and didn't feel like explaining any further. Mostly I wanted to be quiet, and eventually we said goodnight and hung up.

After I ate, I went upstairs, took a sleeping pill, and got into bed. I read for a while waiting for the pill to take effect because I did not want to lie in bed with visions of Susan going around and around in my head.

SIX

BUSINESS WAS SLOW the next morning at the gym. Charlene wanted to know what we were going to do, so I asked, "What do you mean what are we going to do?"

"You know. About Susan," she said.

"There's nothing to do."

"Oh, yes there is."

"Like what?" I asked again.

"Like finding out what happened. What did Susan get herself into? Or was her death a random act? How 'bout an accident? Did she have an accident or did someone cause her to have an accident? Then run away."

"For a few days there's nothing to do while the police investigate. They want to go through her locker here and check her training schedule. They contacted her mother and went through her apartment. The forensic guy hasn't completed the autopsy yet, and we have no information."

Charlene replied, "I bet we can find out a lot of stuff."

"Oh my gosh, Charlene! Leave it alone! Let the police do their job."

Bob came up to the front desk from one of the multi-purpose rooms. He was looking bad – down and morose.

"What is up with you?" I asked.

"You know Susan and I were kinda close."

"How close?"

"Close."

"Don't tell me it was you two in the stairwell," I said.

His eyes got huge. "How did you know about that? Well, we weren't the first ones to start it."

"I am so sorry you have lost a good friend, Bob." He actually cried for a few minutes. Charlene handed him a tissue and a donut.

"We have got to find out what happened," he said.

"Not you too! Look, there's nothing to do. We need to wait until the police finish their investigation or come up with something."

Even Tiger Lady didn't draw a crowd today. How inconvenient for her. She had difficulty with the drop in her numbers.

Routine investigation tasks began to take place. Detective Andrews went through Susan's locker and got a copy of her training schedule for a month prior and what was booked in the future. Sadly, Susan's mother came in from out of town that afternoon. We had not met before.

"Susan was happy to be working here. She spoke highly of the place and the people she worked with. She had a passion for personal training."

Charlene wanted to know if her mother had thought of anything that might have caused someone to want Susan dead. Susan's mother couldn't think of anything at all, but she did mention that Susan had confidential relationships with her clients and would never really talk about any of them, by name anyways. We helped her gather up Susan's personal clothes and equipment and walked her to the door.

"Can we help with anything you need to do?" I asked.

"I'm going to leave everything of hers the way it is until the police come up with what happened. Would you mind keeping the key of her condo in case I call and need something? I'm staying at a hotel until the autopsy is done and they release her body, then I am planning a service here since this is where her life was and where her friends are. The local funeral home, Bertrams, has been very helpful, but of course, they handle deaths for a living."

"We're so sorry this happened. It doesn't seem right that a daughter precedes her mother in death," I said. She shook her head, tears running down her face, and left.

Before we closed up for the night, Detective Andrews came by to tell us the results of the autopsy.

"Blunt trauma to the head."

"So it's not accidental?" asked Charlene.

"Unfortunately, not a chance. Nothing personal though."

"Nothing personal!" Charlene's voice was loud and angry. "How can you say that being killed is nothing personal?"

"I just meant that the method of killing is sometimes telling. Depending on the wounds, we can tell if the killer was directly involved with the victim. This was the least personal way to kill, almost like the killer didn't really want to."

"That's a calming thought; hard to take death back. Was it random?" I asked.

"That we don't know. There were no personal belongings at the scene. We found a purse and set of keys at her condo."

"Will you let us know when you get more information from the investigation? I feel like we are personally involved," I said.

"I'll do what I can, but I need to ask you where you three were on Tuesday between noon and four."

"We were all right here and I guess we are each other's alibis," I said.

"I won't accept you vouching for each other. Come up with someone that doesn't work here that could have seen each of you here during that time. I'll check up with them tomorrow."

As he left, Charlene said, "Boy, he's got a lot of nerve!"

Well, I knew I had taken a late lunch and walked to the sandwich shop. There was some of that time that no one I knew saw me. Charlene was at the front counter most of the time, especially while I was gone for lunch. I guess she could have slipped out before or after, but unlikely. I think I would have noticed her absence, but she needs another person to vouch for her. According to the schedule, Bob had clients, but they were not back-to-back time wise. We could check the roster to see who checked in and out of the gym between twelve and four. Those members would have seen us for the time they were in the facility. I'm not sure anyone noticed the three of us long enough to account for every minute of the four-hour timeframe. We were all just around the gym during that time.

SEVEN

SUSAN'S MEMORIAL SERVICE was scheduled for the following Tuesday, exactly one week since we had last seen her. Thank God for Sundays. OverTheTop is closed on Sundays and I wanted to clear my mind for the day. Let's see... what are mind-clearing activities?

- Sleeping in if you are really sleeping and not letting thoughts run through your mind
- Yoga breath
- Yoga
- Going through a gratitude list
- Taking a walk
- Taking a walk with the dog
- Jogging till your mind is clear
- Reflecting on nature
- Praying

- Sitting in the sun on the patio swing reading a book even if you have to wear a coat or blanket
- Talking to a best friend

Max was back in town and came out to ask if I was all right. And I was. I was just processing and coming to terms with what had happened.

He left to ride his bicycle with his bike group. The group only rides four very specific times a week, and it is difficult for Max to be available at those exact times. Hey, if cycling reduces his stress, I'm all for him riding. Having someone sit around just to watch me is not on my list of mind-clearing activities.

Later that evening, we decided to watch a movie as a means of distraction. We didn't discuss the murder much more than exchanging information. Max doesn't speculate often, which is a good thing in this case. Sometimes our minds can be our own worst enemies; self-doubt is a good example. Speculation can be a lot of thought and worry about past and future events that never take place. Time to give thinking a break.

I jogged to work on Monday. We live about three miles from OverTheTop. The sky was overcast and more leaves were turning colors. I needed tights and a jacket to run outside. I showered when I arrived, changed into my traditional spandex outfit, and got ready to open the doors. I told Charlene and Bob to take the day off. I didn't think starting a big marketing campaign was appropriate until after things settled down, but activity sure was slow, especially for a Monday.

Later in the day, the mailman left the mail on the corner of the counter. I noticed there was a letter addressed to Susan. The postmark was MidTown, so the letter was probably for business. But, since I do watch TV, I put on a pair of gloves like the ones we use when we pick up dirty towels before I touched the letter. I wasn't sure if it was okay or not, but I opened the envelop. In big strong printed letters the paper inside read, "You know you can never say a thing." That seemed like a threat. I immediately called the police so they could pick the letter up as evidence. I was kinda wishing to have a day with no big drama. What could that mean – You know you can never say a thing? What did she know? And whom did she know it about? Since the letter came here, it occurred to me that her death might somehow be related to the gym. But how and why?

OverTheTop was closed Tuesday morning during the memorial service for Susan, which was held at the United Church of Christ in downtown MidTown. The interior of the building was dark with wood pews, burgundy carpet and stained glass windows. Susan's mother and her stepdad were there. I realized that Susan never mentioned her real dad. Many of her friends attended the service, and I recognized a lot of members and clients from work, including Mick Ballard. The pastor and Susan's good friend, Sarah, eulogized her with meaningful remembrances of her life.

After the service, we drove to the graveside ceremony in the cemetery on Second Street. The grave was prepared with green artificial turf around the hole in the ground. Seeing the casket lowered into the ground made me realize Susan was cheated and that her death was very final.

That afternoon Detective Andrews stopped by and told me the letter had no finger prints, but pointed in the direction of this being a premeditated or impulse killing.

"What is an impulse killing?" I asked.

"One where the killer impulsively decided there was no other way."

"Do you think it could be related to the gym?"

"There's really no way to tell yet. But be careful and mindful of what you do. If something seems suspicious, stay away and call me." He handed me a card with his cell phone number, then left.

"What the hell is going on?" asked Charlene. "This is getting weirder by the minute."

"We need to respect Susan's death, but we need to try to stay positive in life. The more positive energy you have, the more you get. Positive attitudes lead to success," I said, trying to convince myself that was the answer.

"Alright, Halloween's comin' up. I'll decorate the bulletin board with black cats. And you know all those photos you took of the fall colors? Let's get a couple framed and hang those up."

As the week went on, clients either cancelled appointments they had with Susan and wanted a refund, or they rescheduled with another trainer. The business was still okay, but just paying the bills, so Joe beefed up our online marketing to grab the attention of potential members.

"The sooner this gets resolved, the sooner we can get back to business because people will know it had nothing to do with the gym," I said.

I figure the demographics of our members extend out three to five miles from our location at most. Not everyone will know what happened.

"I know what we can do! Tomorrow let's retrace her steps!" Charlene declared.

"We did retrace her steps, literally. That's why we found her body!"

"I mean, let's make a timeline of her activities and piece together the last day of her life."

EIGHT

FRIDAY MORNING, CHARLENE, Bob, and I huddled around the front desk. The sky was gray and the temperature warm, like an Indian summer day. When business was slow, we brainstormed what happened on Susan's last day.

"You know with Susan's disappearance and murder, I forgot to tell you that I am one of the lucky people living in the apartments that were being charged $50 more a month than the corporate owners thought we were being charged. Just say this one organization owns 1,000 apartments. That times 50 makes $50,000 a month! Our rent is not going down because the corporate people say we agreed to and signed the lease for the higher rent. Go figure," said Charlene.

"Lucky you," said Bob.

I said, "Okay, let's make a list of what we know...We asked Susan about Mick, she went to get coffee...What was she wearing?"

Charlene said, "When we found her, which was just one week ago today, by the way, she was wearing running clothes, blue shorts, a red shirt, and neon green Newton running shoes."

I thought out loud. "So she must have walked to her condo, dropped off her purse and keys after she got coffee. She changed clothes. Do you think she went jogging alone or with someone? The coffee barista said she spoke to someone on the way out the door, but who knows if she went with anyone? She needed to be back here by 2 pm to keep her appointment with Helen. Anything else you can think of?"

We were stuck there. We could only speculate further because we didn't have many facts.

A Zumba class was running. Listening to some of that upbeat music will get you going. I liked to look around the class because many of the members had smiles on their faces. Zumba somehow got people to come to the gym who wouldn't ordinarily go to a group fitness class. There was something about Zumba that appealed to members who liked to dance. Once you learned the music and the steps, you could workout harder because you weren't anticipating what movements came next. I was a licensed Zumba instructor, but had a long way to go to shake, pump, and thrust convincingly. Zumba doesn't feel natural to me. Max often teased me and wanted me to practice on him.

Zumba was definitely one way to attract more members. Becca looks down her nose at Zumba. If she would promote it in any way, I know a lot of her following would try the class. After Zumba, Becca would teach her hi-lo aerobics class followed by a strength class. Members were happy.

Charlene manned the front counter while Bob and I worked with clients. Sam Good arrived causing Charlene to perk and drool. Sam and I met back in one of the multi-purpose training rooms. He was very sympathetic about the loss of Susan and the shock of finding the body. He presented a shoulder for me to cry on, but I wasn't going to take his offer. His body was awfully close to mine and he smiled slightly, like an invitation. Yikes, I thought. There was definitely some heat going on in this training session. I felt a little vulnerable, so I got busy. We increased the weight and decreased the reps for his triceps this week. He was lifting heavy and sweating heavy too. I suddenly wondered – was there DNA in sweat?

After he went to the locker room, I said, "Charlene, you cannot be so obvious and drool so much when Sam comes in! Act polite, friendly, and professional! He will think highly of you."

"Wanton is the way I want him to think," she replied.

After we closed the gym for the night, Max was waiting at home with grilled brats and sweet potato fries. He's a man after my own heart. After we ate, we decided to 'go upstairs' early. Snuggling and spooning throughout the night felt good. I like the feel of his naked body against mine. Talking isn't all it's cut out to be especially when you can just hold each other.

NINE

SATURDAY WAS WARM for October. There was a light breeze and the leaves rustled on the sidewalk as I jogged to work. The smell of leaves changing color and drying out filled my breath. I was wearing shorts, a t-shirt, and of course, my sunglasses. When I went shopping for sunglasses, I spent a long time finding just the right ones. They had to be 'cool,' fit my head, and accommodate bi-focal lenses. Arriving at the gym, I showered and put my workout gear on for the day. People who know me never say I am a great dresser because they rarely see me in street clothes.

Charlene rushed in with her bag of glazed chocolate donuts. She threw them on the counter and ran close to me.

She whispered, "Do you believe in ghosts?"

"Really, Charlene? You have got to be kidding! She's only been in the ground a couple of days."

"When do you think ghosts start haunting, anyways? I've heard that some of them don't know how to communicate with people right away. Maybe we could find out what happened from her. Do you believe in them?"

I said, "I believe in something more than coincidence. But I am not one of those people who can hear and see spirits. MidTown historically has lots of hauntings."

"Seriously, where?"

"There are supposedly several hauntings downtown on Jeffrey Street and nearby. A female ghost in a long dress can be seen looking out of a second story window. One of the restaurants has a woman's name etched with a diamond on a windowpane. Then there's Ackerman Cemetery near Chester that's very old but mostly locked up. Ghosts are seen floating over tombstones there around Halloween. And of course the very cemetery Susan is buried in has been reported to have ghost lights. The ghost tours pick up this time of year because of Halloween coming up. There are walking tours and trolley tours."

"Maybe if we go to her grave," Charlene said, "we can see or feel her."

"Why do you think she would show up there and not here or at the Riverwalk? Or how about her apartment?" I asked.

"I guess cos her body's there, or do they haunt where they were killed? Maybe ghosts haunt only those who can help them with unfinished business."

"I don't know. What evidence says that ghosts haunt near their physical bodies or where they died? Does evidence exist that they are real?"

"Don't worry. I'll talk you into going to check in with Susan," said Charlene.

Today I was trying to set up a speaking engagement for next month, mailing out free trial cards to try to bring in new members, and, of course, calling my networking friends and try to get some leads. I'm sure most of them will ask about Susan. Oh, the torture of trying to keep a new business going. I'm not much of a sales person and would rather people just come in and sign up. I can provide great customer service after that point!

The phone rang; Tiger Lady was calling. I mean Becca. She was hysterical. She was biking late in the afternoon yesterday and fell off her bike and broke her collarbone and wrist when her shoe didn't unclip from the pedal. She fell from a curb and had several bruises. She and I talked quite a while as I tried consoling her and asking about her injuries. For the first time since I've known her, she was actually almost real, not superior or superficial. She was concerned for her classes and all the followers who counted on her. She was lost because fitness classes are the life she identifies with. If she wasn't their idol, what was she? Slowly her uptight demeanor returned, and she was positive again because people got through things like this. She planned to stop in when she could move around better.

I spent a lot of the day trying to get instructors to commit to teaching her classes. There are two sides to this equation. The members are snooty and won't be happy with anyone else and will treat the instructor who steps into Becca's spot poorly. However, the classes are big and give the instructors a large ready-made audience, which was a chance to show off and make some converts.

OverTheTop has a lot of good instructors. A few of the newer ones need some practice, but most instructors would jump at the chance to pick up some prime time classes, even temporarily. Guessing she would be out about ten weeks, I scheduled Kathy, Sharon, and Barb to pick up the majority of the classes.

OverTheTop certainly didn't seem to be in the positive energy zone this week. I can't be pulled into thinking negatively, though, because negative vibes will find their way into my life. I have to believe there is a reason for this new twist in fate.

"I don't mean to sound callous," said Charlene, "but what is this going to do for business?"

My thoughts exactly.

"Members aren't going to cancel just because their favorite instructor is out for a couple of months. They wouldn't get to see her again, unless she taught somewhere else. Uh, oh. Perish the thought. Exercise and fitness are important in their lives regardless if they become accustomed to a particular instructor or not. Besides, they will realize that taking someone else's class is great for cross training."

Max picked me up at the end of the day. We planned to grille shrimp and vegetables and eat a kale salad. The weather was too nice out to have soup even though it was October. We were lucky to have this little bit of summer again before winter hit.

He told me about his morning bicycle ride with the group. The weather was still good enough for road rides and twenty people showed up. I always think trust is a big issue in cycling. If someone doesn't know or follow the rules for riding in a group, a bunch of people could get hurt.

I told him about Tiger Lady and her injuries. OverTheTop instructors are good, and I feel confident that the subs will wow the classes. Max usually agrees with my choices because he is not intimately involved with the business.

Thank goodness tomorrow is Sunday.

TEN

MY CELL PHONE rang before I got out of bed. I dashed for it because I rarely get called at home. Detective Andrews was on the line.

"Oh no, what do you want on a Sunday morning?" I asked.

"There's been an incident at OverTheTop."

"An incident? What the heck is an incident?" I asked.

"There's been some vandalism. Someone spray painted a symbol by the entry way in red paint."

"A symbol? What kind of symbol?"

"It's a big NO sign. Like the red circle with the diagonal line running through it."

"Are there any words?" I asked.

"No, just the symbol."

"I'll be right over."

Max drove over with me, and as we got out of the car, sure enough, we saw a big red circle spray painted with a diagonal line through it. I shouldn't have been surprised, but actually seeing the symbol made a big impact. The vandal looked like he was trying to stop people from coming to the gym or to warn someone off. Who knows? The damage was visible for everyone to see.

"Do you think this has anything to do with Susan's death?" I asked Detective Andrews.

"We can't discount the possibility," he said.

Wow! That was a profound statement and helpful too! I am really annoyed about not getting answers from him!

I called around and found a company that could come and power wash the building. They couldn't promise the paint would come off completely, but would do their best. How about sand blasting? The wall was brick after all. Was the paint oil based or latex?

"Their job is to remove the paint. Let them worry about it now." I was frustrated.

"Max," I said, "things are just getting weirder and weirder. I'm not sure what's happening, but I feel like I have to find out."

"It will be alright," he said. "We'll figure it out." I was surprised he was acting reassuring. Sometimes reassurance is all a person needs. Max tends to want to take action more than reassure.

OverTheTop

Max is a co-owner of a manufacturing company in Allsburg. Allsburg is the next town west of here. The location is a little more industrial, but has neighborhoods too. He runs the engineering and installing side of the company, and his sidekick Stew runs the marketing and sales side. The two of them talk about everything, even worse than some women do.

Stew is the one who came up with the name OverTheTop. He researched names and functions of similar companies and somehow put the company name together.

Max is more like an engineer. He knows all the nuts and bolts, all the processes, and all the assembly information. His business is alien language to me until I see the end products, and then I understand how everything works. Not really. But I get the flow. The company couldn't run with out Max; no one understood the whole picture and all the pieces but him.

However, Stew could schmooze and coddle almost anyone, and that was not Max. Stew knew a lot of people and held court in cigar bars and regular bars. His family included a few policemen from the south side. After Stew told them the situation, they recommended using a private detective and gave him the name of one in particular. I didn't want to hire someone for a full out investigation, but if this person could add a little more information than the police here seemed to be able to find, I'd be happy to hear it. Her name was Michelle, Mitch for short.

Stew's brother called her and gave her the basic information about Susan and the vandalism at the gym. She headed my way, from where I don't know. When she arrived, I detailed everything that had happened to date. She listened well, asked few questions, handed me her card, and left to go detect whatever she was going to detect. Mitch had reddish brown hair and was medium height. She was slim and wore khaki pants with a button down shirt. I didn't know much about her, except that she came highly recommended.

So now I'm paying two people, the sand blaster and the detective, Mitch.

# ELEVEN

ON MONDAY, MY daughter, Marissa, was starting work at the gym. She works as a technology consultant who goes to people's homes and businesses and helps them install software and computer systems, then trains them to start using applications and the equipment. She was freelancing and helping me now. I stopped by to pick her up from her apartment, and we drove in together.

She was going to take all the confidential client paper files and digitalize them by creating a database to keep the information secure but searchable. She was also going to create a new member lead database and a current member database so all the information would be in the same format and easily accessible.

Marissa is very conscientious and reliable. I feel comfortable having her work for me and know that she will do a good job. Marissa is from a younger crowd so I was excited to get her perspective on what would draw her crowd to the gym.

As we drove towards the parking lot, I decided the sand blaster people did a pretty good job. I saw some of the graffiti simply because I knew it was there, but was hoping no one else would notice. We went inside and started to get Marissa set up to work.

Charlene busted through the front door, "What in the world is that circle on the building?"

"Oh, please. I was hoping no one would notice," I said,

"Well, the spot is cleaner than the rest of the building, so it is noticeable."

I told them about the vandalism yesterday.

"We should put something festive in that spot then. That will give the clean part a chance to get dirty again," I said.

Charlene put her donuts down on the counter and gave Marissa a hug.

"How you doing'?" Charlene asked.

"Fine, thank you. Happy to be working," Marissa said.

"Well you sure have the talent to be working on these computers. Let me unlock the files and let's set your computer up where no one can disturb you or see what you are doing."

Charlene and Marissa went about setting up a workstation for Marissa. Then Charlene left to go get fall decorations like, hay, corn stalks, and pumpkins to put next to the building out front.

Over The Top

I described the job I needed Marissa to do.

"You need to enter clients by last name first. Enter the health history. Activity history. Goals. Progress reports. Any fitness assessment scores with the dates. Any notes added by the trainer or special considerations. Date everything. And remember that what goes on at the gym stays at the gym."

"Mom," she said, "you know I get all that confidentiality stuff."

"Oh, and create a backup plan for the files," I said.

I watched as she started working. Where she got her soft, curly, brown hair from, I'll never know, but she looked beautiful.

Bob came in with his interesting (sometimes) bit of trivia. "Why are flamingos pink?" he asked.

"What in the world does that have to do with anything?" I asked.

"Just answer."

"Dunno."

"Because they eat shrimp."

"Huh, never knew that," Marissa said.

Charlene returned and attractively arranged our festive decorations, including bales of hay, some corn stalks, Indian corn, gourds, and pumpkins, just over the clean spot on the building.

She shared her donuts with Bob and Marissa. I mentioned hiring a detective to find some additional information about Susan, the letter, and the graffiti. I wanted Mitch to try to figure out if any of the incidences were related.

"Did you tell her about us retracing Susan's steps?" asked Bob.

"Yes, I told her everything that we know and what we did. She didn't ask many questions, but seemed to know how to get answers."

Members were coming in for the Monday morning step class. Bob's first client arrived. Marissa entered data. Charlene manned the front desk. And I tried to do what I was supposed to do on Saturday before Becca called about her big injury. Marketing. I got the free trial cards ready to mail and left messages at two different organizations trying to set up speaking engagements. Lunch came and went. The group of us ordered from the fast sandwich place around the corner. I got a lettuce wrap with turkey and cheese, potato chips, and a diet coke fountain drink.

Noon classes ran – a strength class and an interval class for older adults. The gym was generally quieter in the afternoon, but members that did not like to be here during busy or crowded times regularly showed up in the afternoon between one and four.

Later in the day, Mitch came in. She has a quality entrance. She wasn't there and suddenly she was there, like she quietly slipped in as if to go unnoticed. She told us she followed up with the police and repeated the steps we thought Susan took.

"The lady in the coffee shop saw her around 11 o'clock. Susan did talk to a man as she left on her way out the door. His back was to the counter so the barista did not see his face. Susan was not in the clothes she had on at the gym. Evidently, she stopped by her condo and changed clothes before heading out to the Riverwalk where she was probably walking or jogging. No murder weapon was found, but the injury would be consistent with a large rock; any rock in the river could be the weapon. The murder seems to have been done quickly with out much thought. I mean how could a murder take place in the middle of the day on the Riverwalk, and no one notices?"

"The letter that was mailed here could be related to her death, not sure yet, but very coincidental if it's not. Maybe the killer was warning her off of something and then decided to kill her before she got the threat in the mail. Also, the vandalism could be just that, but very coincidental if it was. Becca's injury? Haven't figured out a tie in for that yet."

"Wow. That just about covers it," I said. "You gave us a lot of new and old information. What's next?"

"Well, if I figure anything out, I will let you know," Mitch said, and quietly left.

We were pretty speechless. Poor Marissa. She was sitting in on the conversation and had no idea the extent of the situation until now.

Late afternoon I drove Marissa home, letting Bob and Charlene close up. Marissa talked about everything that happened to make some sense out of the confusion.

After I dropped her at her apartment, I drove home and took Matt for a walk. I was in shorts and a t-shirt with my fanny pack that carried a plastic bag in case I had to poop scoop. Matt is a Husky and a huge attraction for kids. They say, "Oh! A husky" or "Look! A snow dog!"

We were walking on the sidewalk in the neighborhood and I was collecting different leaves. I picked up different colors and shapes. I also got some of those little helicopters and acorns. When we got back home from the walk, I arranged the leaves on the grass to overlap each other in a nice design. I added the helicopters and acorns to the top of the pile.

Using my digital camera, I zoomed in on the leaves and took several macro shots. Sprinkling the design with drops of water changed the whole effect. I love photography, but don't always have the time or inclination. We hung some similar shots I took up on the wall in the gym as decoration for the season. The framed photos are part of our attempt to be festive.

Matt lay in the grass totally appreciating my artwork and me.

TWELVE

ON TUESDAY, INTUITION, or a nagging feeling, prompted me to go back to the scene of the crime. The weather was still warm, but overcast. I parked at the gym and walked down the street to the Riverwalk and went south almost until the bike path hooked on to the trail. Bicycles are prohibited on the part of the Riverwalk closest to town. Funny, because I saw bike tire tracks along the side of the brick pavers.

Through the bushes and trees was the crime scene, the place we found Susan. The crime tape was gone, and I walked down a few steps to the river. The water was flowing past with a gurgling, strong current, but wasn't very deep as it bubbled over rocks along the way. Life was going on as if nothing happened. I could hear the quiet in the air along with the rushing of the water. What an eerie feeling to know Susan died in this same space two weeks ago. My eerie feeling increased as I imagined someone else was close and observing. I'm watching too much TV I guess, although I don't watch very often.

Back at the gym, life went on too. Bob came up to me and asked me what the first capital of the United States was.

"Dunno," I said.

"Philadelphia."

"Huh," I said.

I wondered if he was this clever with his clients. No one seemed to avoid him.

Charlene brought in chocolate covered éclairs. Marissa was working on the client files, and I ended up teaching a step class for Becca because Sharon, the sub, had a sick child. So I was the sub of the sub. What a way to go! They thought I did fine! I am a good instructor. Teaching takes more thought when you don't do it regularly, but I had a few 32 count choreography segments memorized from using them over the years.

Bob was training the new client, Beth McMan, when I finished working with Helen, the young red head that was supposed to start with Susan. She had an upbeat personality and appeared to be as tough as nails, in charge, and a go-getter. No one was bringing her down. She physically wanted strength and definition.

Then along came Sam Good, and I introduced him to Helen. Charlene was behind him silently waving her arms and mouthing "No." I asked Sam and Helen if they knew Charlene to bring her into the conversation. We just small talked about the weather and working out, polite conversation formalities. The kind of sayings like "How are you?" "Fine." Why do we do that to each other? Most people could care less.

As we dispersed, I walked back to the personal training area to meet Sam when he came out of the locker room. Today we were going to increase resistance and reduce reps for biceps. He was building muscle as we continued with the program, that's for sure. He talked about his weekend and running along the MidTown River Bike Trail. "Do you want to meet me out there sometime?" he asked.

"Maybe we could get a group together to meet out there for a special event," I replied.

"Not what I meant."

I thought – smartass.

"I know. Keep lifting."

He smiled slightly, that invitation still in his eyes. I smiled slightly back and batted my eyelashes to add humor to the moment.

On weeknights the gym closes at 7:30 PM. Just to stir things up, Charlene convinced me to walk over to the MidTown Cemetery and go by Susan's grave. This certainly turned out to be a day for reflection! As we walked up the road towards the grave, I asked Charlene if she was getting any ghost vibes.

"Don't you make fun of me! It's not respectful of the dead!"

We stood by the grave. Engraved granite markers took several weeks to make, so we were looking at a patch of dirt about the size and shape of a coffin. Leaves were rustling in the breeze, the crisp fall air surrounding us like a shroud. Suddenly the sound was an awful lot like rustling footsteps in the leaves and not the breeze. We got spooked and took off running down the hill till we got to the sidewalk. Were the footsteps real or ghostly?

"We have got to quit acting like we just watched a scary movie!" I said.

We spooked as we scurried back to my car, then I dropped Charlene off at her apartment.

I was going home to Max and Matt. That felt comforting and safe to me. I often have conversations with the dog, but no way was I talking about ghosts and spooks with Max.

THIRTEEN

THE REMAINDER OF the week started an upward trend. Business increased and the revenue and cash flow was positive! Some of the free trial postcards came in and potential members took promotional classes. The Friday Zumba class was popular, as well as, the hi-lo and strength classes that followed. Kathy subbed both of Tiger Lady's classes.

As she left the building, she smiled and said, "I think they liked me! They were surprised that they would, but they did!"

"Congratulations," I said. "That's one tough diehard crowd to win over!"

Marissa was pitching in at the front counter and answering phone calls when we needed help. She was getting caught up in the business of the gym. You have to love fitness to be in the industry. For most people there's no way to make a full time living at fitness because of personal physical constraints (you can only teach so many classes) and the availability of clients (you seldom have too many). Individual expenses are high for instructors, like certifications, clothes, music, continuing education, and shoes. Fortunately the gym had all of the equipment for personal training, but being outfitted came at a high cost. OverTheTop was doing well again.

Friday night after I went home, Max and I were getting ready to eat some chili cooked in the crockpot. The weather started cooling off and chili seemed like a good idea. Chili, soup, crock pot food all went together with colder weather. The days were getting shorter and nights were getting dark sooner.

I heard someone banging on the door, looked out the window, and saw Genna, the 'mean neighbor,' just what I needed today or any day. Her medium height, brown hair chopped off at chin length, and hard angry look were very familiar to me. What does that woman want to complain about now? I opened the door and she said, "You better get your cat under control. It's snarling and making all kinds of racket, and I just can't have that."

"We don't have a cat," I replied.

"Well it's up in your tree. Fit to be tied."

Thankfully she left before I gave her something fit to be tied over. I could hear a lot of snarling and scraping and walked into the front yard. Sure enough, in the tree, scrambled a huge black cat, glowering and clamoring, running around branches, screeching, snarling, and flipping.

"Max, bring a flashlight out here," I yelled. When Max walked into the front yard, we looked up into the tree and saw the cat twisting and turning on a very short leash tied to the tree.

"What do we do? How do we get it down? It's going to attack anyone who gets close. The cat may hang itself on that leash. Who tied it there? And how did no one see it happen? And why? Why did someone tie it there? Whose cat is it?" I fired away asking questions, not waiting for any answers. "It's going to be dead before anyone can get here to help us."

Max went in the garage and calmly put on his leather gloves and hunting coat, got a ladder and a sharp knife (Cutco knife, my favorite). He placed the ladder on a branch on the other side of the tree from the cat. The ladder was about two feet from the trunk as he reached across and sliced the leash that was tied on the tree. The cat dropped to the branch below and down to a lower branch, jumped to the ground, and ran through the neighbors' bushes, never to be seen again.

"Thank you for gearing up and taking care of the situation. I remember when you suited up to find Matt when he ran away in the blizzard. You were a hero then too. That poor cat. What do you think is going on?" I was rambling, rambling.

"Could just be a prank. Halloween is coming up in two weeks," said Max.

"Could be someone doesn't like me! What if this is related to the vandalism at the gym?"

Max said, "I just can't say. I don't know."

"Well, I don't really believe in coincidences! Should we call the cops? What if the vandalism was related to Susan? Could this all be a warning?"

"The cat is gone and hopefully safe, although scared to death. Since it could just be a prank, let's leave it alone unless something else happens," said Max.

"It's freezing out here. Although, going in and eating doesn't sound terrific at the moment," I said.

"Our chili is always terrific," Max said as he walked away to put the ladder and his gloves back. The Cutco knife belongs in our kitchen.

I didn't have a clue what was going on, I only had questions.

FOURTEEN

BUSINESS ON SATURDAYS at the gym was always brisk. As I drove to work, the rain started, and I knew we would be very busy. I pulled up my hood and rushed from the car to the building. Charlene was already inside with mini éclairs. Now if I had a bag of those, I would eat them all, or have to throw them away, or put them down a garbage disposal to stop myself.

"Did you see that Charles Johnson is running an ad campaign promising to beat our prices at PowerUp?" she asked.

"That feels personal. Did he specifically say OverTheTop or just beat the price of the competition?" I asked.

"He said OverTheTop."

"Huh. Seems to me that they have quite a large membership enrolled. Why would they want to pinpoint our gym?"

"It's not personal. It's business," Charlene said.

Mick Ballard came in for a training session with me. He talked about how odd he felt to have Susan gone and to be using another trainer. Odd is a good description. Her presence is around us. We were in the same air that she breathed too. I gotta stop having these thoughts! I went through Mick's folder to see what he had been working on and asked him questions about his goals and what he wanted to walk away with from his sessions. We did a lot of chest work: chest presses, push ups, bench presses. The embezzlement case he was involved with was never discussed.

After Mick finished training, I checked my voicemail, and Susan's mother had left a message asking if I would go to Susan's condo to check up, just to make sure there was no mail and that everything was in working order. She wanted the heat turned on in case we got a frost. I made a mental note to go later in the day when business had settled down a little bit. The next message was a hang up.

Marissa was working at the front counter checking people in and out and answering the phone.

"Mom, we have had four hang ups just this morning," she said. "That's unusual."

"What did the caller id say?" I asked.

"Unknown."

"Huh."

We ordered in super fast sandwiches for lunch with chips and pickles, and, of course, fountain diet diet cokes, for Bob, Marissa, Charlene, and me. As we ate, I told everyone about the black cat story. They all agreed that the incident was beyond explanation, having no suggestions about how, why, or what to do. What happened is a jaw dropper, disbelief that something like that actually occurred.

"You know, they say that when some one abuses animals as a child, they grow up to abuse people as adults and may be violent," Marissa said.

"Good to hear. That's comforting," I said, "along with all the superstitions about black cats. Let's hope this black cat represents luck and prosperity instead of an evil omen."

I told them all the questions I wanted answers to, but everything we talked about was just speculation, which usually leads no where. I decided to call Mitch later, since we hadn't talked to the police, to have her put the cat event into the mixing bowl of information, whether it turned out to be connected in any way to the vandalism or Susan.

Leaving Marissa and Charlene in charge, I walked over to Susan's condo with a raincoat on. I went to the third building and opened the mailbox for #3C. There were a few bills, junk mail, and a letter. Who writes letters these days with email and texting available? I went to her door and felt like I should be knocking and calling out her name. As I stepped inside, the air felt deathly quiet and cold. I set the thermostat to heat at 65°. The furniture had been shifted around a little, but the police did a thorough search so that was understandable. Because her fridge contained eggs, milk, and some leftover food, I found a garbage bag and threw the old food out. Okay, now this eeriness was spooky. There was definitely a ghostly feeling when being in someone's space that is no longer alive. Talk about breathing the air she breathed! The sheets were stripped from the bed, but the cover was on top of the mattress. The feeling that she would not be sleeping there again was overwhelming. I gotta get out of here, fast!

I threw her trash in the condo dumpster and took her mail back to the gym to put in an envelop to mail to her mom. When I came in, Marissa said she thought that someone was really trying to annoy us because she had five more hang ups. I checked my voicemail and had one hang up message.

I called Mitch and told her about the black cat incident and the hang ups and asked her if there was a way to find out what number the calls were coming from. She said she would check into both issues.

I have had enough of this day. As I was leaving to go home, Charlene said, "Don't forget that next week is the fundraiser raffle for Breast Cancer Awareness Month. We are going to sell raffle tickets for $10 each and raffle off an iPad and 10 personal training sessions."

"Wow. I would have totally forgotten. We have the big glass bowl in the office to put the raffle tickets in, and I will get started on our email marketing campaign. Marketers say that someone may need to see your ad seven times before they pay any attention. Just because the public doesn't respond now, doesn't mean they won't respond later. I think marketing people sell auto-response systems where you can send out weekly fitness tips and monthly newsletters too. Seems like a lot of work to stay current! Have a good Sunday."

Thank goodness for Sundays. I knew there was a reason for a day of rest.

FIFTEEN

ON MONDAY, BOB approached me at my desk in my office at the gym. The office is next to the front counter, a little bigger than a cubbyhole. There's room for a bookcase, two filing cabinets, my desk and chair, and two chairs for visitors. The office door closes, so there is some privacy. He was a little concerned about one of Susan's newer clients who he acquired after her death.

"Every session, he keeps asking questions about Susan trying to find out more information about her life and what happened," he said. "I make my answers short only using information that was made public during the investigation. He wants to know how we feel about her murder and what our thoughts are."

"I wonder what that's all about?" I asked. "Thank you for telling me. Which client is it?"

"He is Bill Moody, and he only worked with her a couple of times. He sure is curious, maybe this is big excitement for his life."

"Does he let on what he already knew or knows about her?"

"Not much, but he does seem to be very familiar with the situation. He knows about when and how she died, where she lived and that she liked the coffee shop. He also knew that she liked to run on the Riverwalk. He asked how the trail was for running. I guess he could have picked most of that up in the news or from her during their training sessions."

"Let me know if he continues to pursue the conversation about Susan. I'm not sure if his interest is out of line because he was her client, and her death was recent."

"Will do."

During lunch I asked Marissa to watch the front counter. Charlene talked me into going to the cemetery again, but this time we were going during the day. We walked down the street to the cemetery and then up the road to Susan's grave. Big oak trees lined the roadway through the cemetery. There was a lone red rose on the dirt at the site of her grave. We were quiet. I think Charlene was trying to tune in and glean some information from ghostly vibes. I was just running good memories through my mind of the time we knew each other. She was a great trainer and added a lot of value to life. I remember her laughter, smile, and positive attitude. I thought it was a shame that her life ended so early. Life was cheated all around by her death.

As we left, Charlene asked if I felt like someone was watching us.

"It does feel odd, but someone is not standing sentry watching everyone that goes to her grave."

"I got a feeling while we were standing there," Charlene said. "But I don't know what the feeling is trying to tell me."

"Maybe your feeling is grief," I replied.

"Maybe somebody is watching us instead," she said.

Back at the gym I had a voicemail from Joe Ellis asking me if I could come by 'his office' sometime today. That was a little unusual because we didn't have any plans to meet or any outstanding work to complete. I called back and told him I had some free time around four o'clock and would drive over then. When I arrived at his house, Joe was definitely angry about something. He started telling me that someone was trying to smear my reputation on the Internet.

"Wait a minute," I said. "What do you mean, smear my reputation?"

"Someone is putting negative comments out about you and OverTheTop."

"Like what? I don't get it."

"Comments about members getting injured regularly, unprofessional training practices, a lot of high fee based classes instead of free classes."

"Can they just do that?" I asked.

"Yes, and worse, they can do that just because they want to ruin your name or your business. I think I got a handle on it so far. One way to help is to reengineer the posts so that so that they go to the back page of search results. People rarely scroll through to the last page of results. That is defensive engineering. Then I make sure your good stuff has first page domination. I did find the IP address that this negative campaign is coming from. I was able to route some of the negative campaign into a "file" that I put out there to contain the comments so they won't go public on the Internet at all."

"Is this illegal?" I asked.

"So many things on Internet law have not been defined. I guess we could find out who is behind the negative comments and go for slander or character defamation. I'm not really sure if there is a course of action we can take at this point. The IP address was from a public computer at a local college so I can't identify an individual that input the comments."

"I only hope I can catch any future action," he added.

"I am definitely being targeted," I said. I told him about the vandalism, the cat, and now the Internet.

"That would be a whole lot of coincidences, if nothing was going on."

"I am calling Detective Andrews and also giving the information to a private investigator called Mitch. If either of them contact you, will you tell them your side of the story?"

"Sure. And I will keep scanning to see if there's any more action."

Back at the gym, I left a message for Andrews, then I called Mitch and filled her in on the latest attack. She was all about me being a target, told me to go on the offense by being aware of my surroundings at all times. She told me that the hang ups were from two different throw away cell phones that were sold in many stores in the area.

Just on a gut feeling, I asked her to check on a person named Bill Moody because he was training at the gym and showed a lot of curiosity about Susan. Mitch warned me to take care again and told me she would be in touch soon.

When I talked to Detective Andrews, he was a little pissed that I had not called him about the cat, but admitted there wasn't enough to go on to include that activity in the investigation at that point. After I told him about the hang ups and now the Internet attack, there was plenty to start an investigation.

So I asked, "What is this? Stalking? Character defamation? Threats? A warning?"

"Well, it's something…Make sure you take care…There has been no physical threat against you so far, but you can not be sure what is on the agenda of whoever is doing this."

OverTheTop

I reiterated the whole situation to Marissa, Charlene, and Bob. We agreed to make some time tomorrow to brainstorm what we thought was happening and who we thought could be responsible.

I was going home to Max and Matt. We walked the dog, breathing in the cool fall air, then ate our famous Spanish pork chops that were cooked in the crock pot. We talked late into the night about memories of vacations, dreams for retirement, and plans to spend time together. We both feel more stress talking about day-to-day aggravations, so our conversations about happy times are relaxing. Relaxation is what I need.

SIXTEEN

I DROVE MY standup car to work Tuesday. There was a chill in the air that felt just like fall. I was trying to figure out how to do more market research, like how to get demographics and what demographics are attracted to our services. OverTheTop was a small neighborhood type gym. We had a nice aerobic studio and ran some great cardio, strength, Pilates, and yoga classes. Other than that we had six multi-purpose training rooms. Each room was equipped with strength and cardio equipment that could be used for personal training. There was a standalone weight machine that regular clients could sign in for specific times to work out between training sessions. We have a nice set up.

PowerUp had a larger weight and cardio room for members and a smaller group fitness class population. Magic Life was huge - all glass and chrome looking - you could see members through the windows working out there at all hours everyday. Some people in our demographics obviously wanted big and shiny and new. Some people wanted more of a neighborhood gym like OverTheTop. There were several more fitness facilities in the area, both larger and smaller. Some were very specific like - Yoga Studio, Personal Training, Pilates Studio.

I looked at the Facebook page of PowerUp and they were definitely challenging our prices, but I wasn't going to reduce membership fees or package prices as a reaction because we have quality at our place. That's our brand - quality. Now I just need to market it! Speaking engagements, articles in the local paper, free trial cards, Internet web page and blog.

Currently, I was trying the email marketing idea. For regular members, we could send monthly tips and a fact sheet detailing special offers, events, and classes. For non-members we could send the same, but ask for an action step for them to commit to coming in and checking us out. Sign up! That's what we really want.

When I entered the gym, Charlene was eating a chocolate covered donut with Bob and Marissa.

Bob asked, "How old is the average turtle before it can reproduce?"

"Dunno," I said.

"25."

"Huh."

"Is the Mick Ballard here the same one that's been in the news about the real estate scam for the past three weeks?" asked Marissa.

"The one and only," I said.

"He sure seems like a cool cucumber. No sweat. No stress. No bags under the eyes," said Marissa.

"You're right. I trained him the other day and he seemed fine. He was appropriately sorrowful and concerned about Susan. Seemed like he really missed her."

"Do you think he's guilty of the rental scam?"

"I have no way of knowing. I was surprised when the story came out, but who's to tell?"

Without even noticing, Mitch made her stealth, quality entrance. She's like a silent intruder, but she's not intruding.

"Do you have any info you can share with me about Bill Moody?" she asked. "I can't find a real Bill Moody anywhere. I even followed him from the gym yesterday, and he led me to a temporary housing hotel. He's registered as Bill Moody, but the trail ends there. There is no license, birth certificate, no record at all."

Marissa pulled up his file. "May I?" she asked me. I nodded. She gave Mitch the address and cell number he listed. "He has a 90 day membership including two training sessions a week. His MasterCard is in the system for auto renewal."

"Hum." She was gone. She left as quietly as she came.

OverTheTop

"It's not like she's creeping," said Charlene, "because she's on our side, right? I've never seen someone come and go like that!"

I spent some time googling OverTheTop and local fitness centers to see if there was any more negative campaigning against us. The Internet seemed calm. I wondered if that was a bad sign because whenever there was calmness lately, some kind of drama started playing out.

Time for Sam Good's training session. He was usually right on schedule. Nothing new today. As he came in and headed to the locker room to get ready, even Marissa stopped in her tracks. I saw her elbow Charlene to try to get her to stop drooling as I went back to the multi-purpose room to get ready to work his lats, rhomboids, levators, and traps today. What a nice part of the body, the back, that is. A little standing work, a little seated work, and a little prone work (face down) is what we did. Between sets, we casually chatted about superficial things in life like his favorite pie that his Grandma makes and what color he wanted his next car to be. When he stood up, I was looking straight into his sweaty pecs. I backed up and he grinned. "If you like what you see, I'm yours," he said.

"Uh, Sam, knock it off! You would hate to ruin a perfectly good client/trainer relationship!"

He smiled again. What a tease!

I know he's teasing me, but why me? Why not Charlene or Marissa? They are available. Maybe that's why. Some guys didn't like availability. Of course, I could just be enough of a hotty to get his attention! And then there's that personal relationship that gets going during training sessions between a client and the trainer. The things we develop in this life! The habits of our minds!

Max and Matt were at home waiting for me. We discussed having peanut butter and fluff sandwiches for dinner, but decided we would have to eat too many to feel full. We had salad with chicken on top instead, and warm bread with butter. Occasionally, we try to stay gluten free, but bread is one food we can't find a good substitute. I remind myself to be very thankful that we are not ill and forced to stay gluten free. We just try to stay healthy.

Max knows I'm a little stressed running the gym, but he knows if I share details with him, he will be stressed more too. He's pretty good at knowing when chilling out is a better option. We watched TV until bedtime, let Matt out before bed, and went upstairs.

SEVENTEEN

I WOKE TO my cell phone ringing. Max was still asleep next to me. The clock on the nightstand next to our bed read 6:15. Charlene and Bob were supposed to open the gym today. What was wrong now? The caller id was Mitch's secret cell number. I answered.

"Can you meet me at the coffee shop in an hour?" she asked.

I said I would be there.

She was waiting for me when I walked in. I ordered peppermint hot chocolate with skim milk, no whip cream. When we sat down she spoke quietly.

"Life is getting interesting," Mitch said.

Okaaaay. What was that supposed to mean?

"I just came from Mick Ballard's place. The police are swarming over there. Apparently, Mick is dead. I hear it looks like suicide, but his death is questionable. The medical examiner will have to state the reason for death."

My head was spinning with even more questions and no answers. What, if anything, did this have to do with me? Other than one of my members was dead? And one of my personal trainers was dead? And they trained together?

Mitch continued stating the facts, "Susan was a personal trainer. Susan was killed. Mick was her client. Mick has been training with you. He may somehow be involved in a big embezzlement scheme. He's dead. This all happened within three weeks."

"And how am I supposed to process all that?" I asked.

"Something big is happening. Something that is bigger than Susan's death. Something that must involve more money than Mick was skimming off the top, if he was. I just haven't figured out what and how you are involved. Do you know or have something that someone wants? All of your incidences seem to be too coincidental for you not to be involved. Do you have a FOID card?"

That question jumped out of nowhere. "Yes, actually. I wanted to learn to shoot for years and Max and I never got around to it."

"I'd like to take you and Max to the range for target practice. You need to be able to protect yourself. Mick was shot. Even if you aren't part of this, better safe than too late."

OverTheTop

What Mitch said got me going, all stirred up. I hate that all these things were happening to me. I hate what happened to Susan and Mick. I wanted to take some control and start making people accountable for causing the deaths and troubles. My yoga practice of non-reaction went right out the window. I called Max and told him about Mick's death. We agreed to meet Mitch at the shooting range off of West Street at 10 o'clock.

Now me with a gun is a scary thing. Just saying. Mitch gave us a SR9 Ruger for practice. American made, seventeen rounds in a cartridge. This gun can be shot with either hand and is good for home defense. I shot five rounds of the seventeen and hit the target once. My hand wasn't steady and my vision was blurry at best. Lining up the three white dots was nearly impossible. The gun had more kick than I thought. Max shot quite well. He used to hunt and handled a gun with ease. I needed a lot more practice. Mitch suggested that we buy a weapon for protection and that we learn self-defense.

I called my son, Steve, and asked him to help me with target practice. Steve shoots regularly. Shooting is a hobby to him. I can't believe I bought him his first gun. I was going to wear my glasses next time and shoot with a steady hand. Although lining up the three white dots with bifocals might still be a challenge. Steve would be patient with me. He usually reserves judgment on most things in life, including me.

I also asked my friend Rachel to personal train with me because she is a professional presenter on women's self-defense. I wanted to practice the techniques and maneuvers I learned so many years ago, but stopped practicing. Over time, I just forgot what to do to protect or defend myself. Okay, so now I'm getting ready to do just that.

Later in the day Max and I went to a sporting shop in Allsburg and bought an SR9 Ruger for the house. We bought a Sig Sauer P238 autoload pistol for me. We picked out a lockable handgun safe, ammunition, and cases. The law states we have to wait 72 hours to actually take the guns home with us.

"How will this gun be helpful to me if it is locked up in the storage unit?" I asked.

"You'll have to carry it."

"Isn't it illegal to carry a concealed weapon?"

"Not anymore, but sometimes the paperwork takes months for approving a concealed carry gun license. In this state, you can transport a gun if it is unloaded and in some sort of case. You can keep the ammunition in the same case, just not in the gun."

I called Mitch and asked if she was sure we weren't going 'over the top' with all this preparation? She was pretty firm about taking preventative measures because getting killed only happens once! There is no second place in death.

When I finally went to the gym, Charlene, Bob, and Marissa told me what they heard about Mick. The news about Mick had gotten out. Their shocked feelings were apparent.

I described target practice and the guns we bought. They presented me with a different protective scenario.

Charlene asked, "Would you actually shoot someone to protect yourself or others? If you have a loaded gun pointed at a person, do you have the gumption to pull the trigger?"

"Hell yay! If you aren't willing to shoot someone, you shouldn't own a gun."

Marissa asked about alternative self-defense methods like pepper spray, tasers, and stun guns. These were all very good ideas and I decided to purchase one of each. My purse, however, would be too big and heavy to haul around anywhere with all of my weaponry.

Bob said, "I'm just not sure I get the connection between you and these two deaths. Maybe Mitch has stirred up a lot of anxiety in you that may not be necessary."

"You're right. I may be paranoid and overreacting. But I want to do something instead of just having things happen in life. Proactive instead of reactive."

"You sound like you're going to lock and load," he said.

"Well, I'm going to try harder to find out what is going on," I said. "Charlene, let's go listen to some ghosts."

The night was dark, but not as dark as it was going to be after daylight savings time changed next weekend. Now Charlene seemed hesitant instead of me.

"Maybe we shouldn't, you know, stir things up," she said. "You know you don't even get your gun for three days. What are we going to do if we find something or someone unusual at the cemetery?"

"What were we going to do the other two times we were here?" I asked.

"Run like hell."

We walked up the road to Susan's grave. The leaves on the trees made a rustling sound as they blew in the wind.

"See, it's a grave. Nothing to it," I said. There was another red rose on the dirt. I thought I saw a shadow run behind a mausoleum that sat under a tree across the road.

"Whoa, did you see something?" asked Charlene.

"Yes, but be quiet and let's move toward the fence." A branch on a tree close by snapped and broke off.

"Yikes! Here's the part where we run like hell."

We turned toward the road and ran right into Mitch.

"Shh."

She motioned to follow her and we quietly made our way to Second Street.

"A man wearing a long black coat was watching you from behind one of the mausoleums. I think he even had those black ear stretching gauges that make holes in your ears larger. I was reminded of watching a scene in a scary movie," she said.

"What are you doing here?" I asked.

"I stopped by the gym and Bob told me where you were headed. How stupid is this? The most important thing you can do to protect yourself is to be aware of your surroundings at all times. Don't go off alone or into a secluded area. A cemetery at night would not be my first choice."

"I had Charlene with me," I replied.

"Big help that was."

After getting back to the gym, I drove home. Max was working late. Poor Matt is not a great watchdog, so I wasn't into going out for another walk tonight. He was happy to see me though, and I let him out into the backyard for a while.

I decided to make chicken divan and rice. That always cheers me up. Warm melted cheese, broccoli, and chicken sounded appetizing. I really wanted to make chocolate chip cookies and eat the dough. I resisted the cookie urge and ate the chicken and rice.

After resisting, I settled for coffee ice cream, mini chocolate chips, and chocolate syrup. I put leftover chicken divan in a container for Max in case he was hungry when he got home, then went to get ready for bed early. The house was quiet, and I was able to settle down and feel safe.

Nancy Klotz

EIGHTEEN

I DROVE TO work on Thursday because the morning was still dark. I opened the gym and in between answering the phone and welcoming members, I worked on my email marketing campaign. I realize we can't control what happens in life, but sometime I have to stop with all the distractions and try to run a business! I checked my email.

A local women's club wanted me to present in early December about avoiding weight gain during the holidays. In my opinion, the holidays start as soon as Halloween is over. It's a shame, but three weeks to Thanksgiving then four weeks to Christmas. Stores have Christmas stuff out in August and September!

Another group related to the school district wanted to start a series of meetings to discuss lifestyle changes and how to make the changes permanent. I was glad to be able to use my life coach skills. This was exciting. Two opportunities for new business and I get to do my favorite things – present and coach. Hopefully I could make a positive impact that would affect someone's life while increasing business for OverTheTop.

Marissa and Charlene were off today. Bob had clients, so I stayed close to the front counter to handle members and clients. Two of our other personal trainers were working today. Some of our trainers pick two or three days a week and book all of their appointments on those days. They may have eight or ten or more clients in one day.

Cindy is short, cute, and bubbly. Clients like her because she is positive and can make them feel successful even if they just reach down to touch their knees. Truly, this is an accomplishment for many people and they appreciate someone understanding their capabilities.

Terry is tall with brown shaggy hair. He is quick to smile and is clearly well defined under his t-shirt. He is very professional and takes care of business when he has a client. Terry does a lot of drills and movements that use multiple joints of the body, works on strength and balance, and improves core stabilization.

Personal training is an amazing profession. Training is not all about athletes and fit people, although they count. Believe me, people like Sam count. It's about people who may not know the basics of exercise or nutrition or people who cannot get themselves up when sitting on the floor or even people that can't balance themselves. The wide variety of needs seems endless. People hire trainers for many different reasons including not feeling comfortable or confident enough to go into a group fitness setting. Our job is helping people with body awareness and improving function in areas like strength, cardiovascular fitness, flexibility, balance, mind/body, or a combination of these things.

Bill Moody came in for a training session with Bob. I sent him to the locker room to get ready because Bob was already back in the training area. I wonder what Bill's story is. Is he on a witness protection program or is he some evil character trying to do away with the human race? He seemed pleasant enough, and his appearance wasn't intimidating. Ninety minutes later, he very politely left the building. He was balding enough to notice, had a rounded face, and was short to medium in height, probable 5"8" or so, stocky. His street clothes were usually casual slacks, a polo type shirt, and a jacket.

The afternoon hours were calm. Bob came out to the counter with his hands behind his back and a big smile on his face.

"Oh no," I said, "not another trivia question!"

"No." He brought his gloved hands out in front of his body. He was holding a single 15 pound weight.

"Okay, I give. I have no idea what you are trying to tell me," I said.

"Before Bill came in, I wiped this weight clean. He used it during his work out. That means we have fingerprints and sweat."

"Bob, is that even legal?"

"Who knows? But we have the info. Where should I put it until Mitch can pick it up?"

We carefully put the weight into an empty box once used to ship hand soap and lotion. I guess TV doesn't give us all the answers, but at least we will know who this guy is even if the evidence can't be admitted anywhere in court.

I called Mitch and told her what Bob did. "Clever, clever guy," she said.

As we were getting ready to close up for the day, Mitch showed up with her usual entrance. She took the box with the weight and disappeared again.

That night, at home, Max and I took Matt out for a walk. We put on headbands and light gloves. The air was crisp and breezy and smelled like fall, almost winter. The moon cast a glowing light on the trees. Life seems so good when we go out and spend time together. I like to think about my gratitude list when we walk. Max and I don't normally have deep emotional conversations. I hold up my own positive energy as a way of enjoying life more. Usually when we walk, jog, or bicycle, we just enjoy nature and each other's company. Our activities are distractions from everyday stress.

NINETEEN

THE AIR IS cheerier with Marissa and Charlene back at work and also smells like chocolate donuts.

Bob walked up to the front counter. "How many calories do you burn chewing gum?'

"Dunno."

"Twenty an hour."

"Huh." Trivia Bob on the job again.

Detective Andrews walked in the door and nodded his head sideways indicating that he wanted me to go sideways too, I guess. When I walked over to him, he told me that Mick Ballard's autopsy showed that with the trajectory of the bullet, it wouldn't have been possible for Mick to hold the gun, pull the trigger, and have the bullet enter his head at that angle.

"Someone really went out of their way to make his death look like a suicide. Although we haven't made much progress on Susan's murder, the attack seems to have happened quickly with no witnesses. We can't be certain if Mick's murder is related because she was just his personal trainer."

"Just his personal trainer?" I asked.

"We haven't found anything else to link the two. But in case there is a link, you should take extra precautions."

"Such as …"

"Don't go anywhere alone. Don't go out at night. Stay away from bad neighborhoods or isolated areas. The standard drill. Let me know if you have any other threatening or harassing incidents."

"Will do. Please keep me in the loop as much as you can."

That's Detective Andrews – a wealth of knowledge. I can tell he's been at his job too long because he can't break instructions down far enough for us first timers to understand terminology like 'the standard drill.'

When he left, Mitch showed up in his place. How does she do that?

"Okay, there you have it," she said.

"Have what?" I asked.

"Two murders that may or may not be related, three threatening type incidences involving you. In another day or so I'll get back any information on

Bill's prints. I'm saving the weight and not running DNA on the sweat yet."

"You know, I wondered if there was any sweat on Susan other than her own. Can that be checked or was that checked?"

"Good question. Although additional sweat could have also have been from her morning clients. I'll try to find out."

Back at the front counter, I told Marissa, Charlene and Bob about Mick's murder, not suicide. I gave them the same safety warnings that were given to me. My friend Rachel came in before we could talk about the possibilities of Mick and Susan connecting in some way. Rachel was here to teach women's self-defense techniques to me, and we moved to an empty multi-purpose room that had some open space so we could practice.

She told me that research indicated preventive measures were the most effective form of self-defense. That way an attack may be avoided.

"If an encounter with an attacker were to happen, your adrenaline would rush and unless you practice maneuvers for years, you probably won't remember many of them. Your mind would blank unless the movement was familiar enough to be a natural reaction. We are going to stick to a few simple but effective moves that you can do to try to stop an attack and get away."

In my case, I think an attack on me would be planned. If I were ever in a situation where it could happen, they would take advantage of it. I need to be ready to strike back and get away.

When we were through self-defense 101, I said goodbye to Rachel after scheduling another session and went to check my voicemail. Susan's mother left a message for me to call her back. We played phone tag, but eventually got in touch with each other a couple of hours later. Sounding upset, she asked me if I remembered sending a letter in Susan's mail to her. When I told her I did, she said that the letter was hand printed in capital letters and said, "OverTheTop is going down." This was the letter that I picked up in Susan's home mailbox.

Geez, what next? I told her I would call Detective Andrews to ask if he could get an officer in her area to pick the letter up to send to him. I thanked her for calling and letting me know about the letter, then left a message for Andrews including Susan's mom's contact information, although he already had it.

Sam Good arrived for a late day training session. I took a few deep, slow yoga breaths to calm down and start to focus on business. Today we were working lower body.

I could just hear Charlene saying, "I bet you're working lower body."

We were working on squats first and then lunges. We used the squat rack and bar bells for the first three sets of squats and lunges. Then we switched to machines for more squats, glutes, hams, and quad work. He sure is strong, and his muscles pump up when they are worked. He's almost like a bodybuilder except his arms still fit next to his body instead of sticking out to the side because of too much muscle mass. Bodybuilders have a slow lumbering swish, swish, swish, walk as their muscle bulk rubs together when they move. Working with Sam definitely took my mind off all the negative energy going around.

"Do you want to meet for a drink when we are through?" he asked.

"Sam, you sure know how to pick up my day. But no thank you."

He smiled slightly. I thought he was shameless, although his asking brightened my day.

After Sam left, looking for some good news, I called my Internet guru, Joe, to see what was happening with my reputation on the Internet. Luckily, he said he had not seen any more negative activity.

What a day! Home again, home again.

"Let's start a fire and make some s'mores," Max said.

We lit the patio heater to help warm the brisk air and started the gas fire pit. S'mores actually taste quite good when we cook them over the fire. We cook marshmallows one at a time, then stack graham crackers, a chunk of chocolate bar, and the marshmallow into a sandwich looking contraption to eat. The marshmallow oozes out the sides of the graham crackers. Tonight we tried to see the stars, but there was so much light pollution, we couldn't see near as many as when we are in the country. The peaceful quiet of the night and sitting together under a blanket with Max helped calm my thoughts.

Nancy Klotz

TWENTY

SATURDAYS ARE USUALLY busier at the gym because all the weekend warriors come out. The warriors say they don't have time for exercise during the week, and they try to get it all in on the weekend. There's two ways to look at the phenomenon. One, injuries abound and the exercise is not consistent enough for improvements, but two, they are exercising. They are moving. I'll take activity over sedentary any day. Classes are full; trainers are working.

The four of us, Charlene, Bob, Marissa, and I, ordered in lunch from the fast sandwich place. They have a good wheat bread, turkey and cheese sandwich. Of course, we got the chips and sodas. Fountain drinks are amazing. There is nothing quite like a fountain drink!

Over The Top

When business slowed down in the afternoon, I decided to go check Susan's condo again. After her mother's phone call, I wondered if I could have missed something important. Opening the mailbox marked #3C, and finding no mail, I went to her door, unlocked it, and stopped dead in my tracks. Her place looked like chaos. Furniture was turned upside down and papers and pictures were strewn across the floors. I looked at her things as best as I could, paying attention to books and journals, trying to understand a reason for this mess.

Going into her bedroom, I saw that the photos were out of the frames and noticed her diary sticking out from under her bed. As I bent down to pick it up, I heard the front door swing open. Looking under the bed, I saw a pair of men's black leather lace-up shoes walk across the living room carpet. As silent as Mitch, I slid under the bed. The shoes came to the bedroom door and stopped. Then they walked to the kitchen. I slipped out from under the bed, scooted through the living room and out the door. I ran down the stairs, around the corner of the next building, and slipped into a front stoop before I stopped.

Listening very closely, I couldn't hear anyone following. I calmed my breath to quiet the noise. I'll have to tell Mitch that her stealth lessons worked. My heart was still racing, and I could hear the beat in my ears. A few minutes later, I heard a car start and saw a dark blue Malibu drive away. I had no way of knowing if the car belonged to black shoes.

Still holding Susan's diary in my hands, I decided to slither and silently slide back to the gym using the back road from Susan's condo. Hugging the tree line, I kept out of site as much as possible. Just like I tell my exercise classes, I could feel my heart coming in line with my breath and my skin cooling off, everything slowing down. But I am hysterical inside. In the lot behind the gym, I sat under a tree and called Mitch and told her what happened. I then called Detective Andrews and told him I was checking on Susan's condo and found mass disarray.

When I went inside, Marissa immediately grabbed me by the arm, took me into my office, and asked, "What is it?"

She's my daughter. I wasn't sure how much to tell her, but Steve is giving me shooting lessons, so I just told her the truth.

"I'm calm now. I'm thankful for breath. Breathing. Calm." And then I was calm.

Bob and Charlene were startled when I told them the news. When we closed up the gym, I drove straight to Allsburg to pick up the guns.

Earlier in the day, Max drove out of town for a weekend installation his company was doing for a customer in Tennessee. I arranged with Steve for target practice the next day.

OverTheTop

Later eating some leftover pasta, Matt and I sat by each other on the floor while I read a book about self-defense. He likes to have his ears rubbed. Rubbing his ears relaxes both of us!

Thank goodness for Sundays.

TWENTY-ONE

STEVE AND I practiced at an outdoor gun range off of West Street. We shot for an hour and were lucky to have the place to ourselves. Steve taught me everything I needed to know about my guns and shooting. Dang! I'm getting good at this! The ground bouncing targets were 10 to 30 feet away because I anticipate a close encounter. Steve set them up to be at different angles to my body so I could try firing while facing several directions in front of me. I used both the automatic Sig and the Ruger and practiced the different loading techniques.

After we finished, we walked back to the parking lot and made plans to meet for target practice again next weekend. Steve got in his car and pulled away. We waved goodbye. I opened the door to my car and started to get in when I saw the gun case on the passenger seat and realized that I left my ammo and guns on the fence posts. So much for gun safety! I jumped out and ran to retrieve them. BAM! My body flew the last ten feet towards the fence. OMG! I was confused. The ground came up and hit me as I saw Steve's car screech back in the lot and heard sirens.

Steve ran to me and started calling "Mom, Mom. Are you okay?" He sounded like a CPR trainer. When I realized that my faithful old 4Runner was blown up, all I could think was, "Now it's getting serious." Nobody messes with my car.

The paramedics checked me out and patched up a couple of scrapes and cuts. They told me my ears would stop ringing in the next few hours. Along came Detective Andrews in his trench coat.

"So you are on missing persons, homicide, and the bomb squad now?" I asked.

"I'm only getting around because you're getting around. Are you okay?"

"A little shocked, but okay. I must be doing something that's messing up someone's plans."

The area was taped off while the bomb squad collected trace evidence. As Steve and I told Detective Andrews what we had been doing prior to the blast, I noticed my license plate in the grass next to the parking lot and ran to retrieve the bent and burned plate.

"That's evidence, ma'am," a sergeant called out to me.

I hung on to that license plate for all it was worth. Andrews shook his head at the sergeant, and he backed off. Andrews told me not to go overboard with the guns. He reminded me of the gun laws for private use. Thanks for that, right? I almost get blown up, and I get a lecture on gun laws. I know he was trying to keep me out of trouble, but I wasn't in the mood.

Steve drove me home and stayed while Marissa came over. I talked to Max on the phone and he was making arrangements to get home.

"At least the guns and ammo are safe," I said. "We still have our protection plan in place."

"Now don't you get crazy with those things. Guns are no guarantee that you will end up on the right side of the grass," Steve said.

Mitch appeared and shook her head at me.

"We have to keep you alive," she said. "I did go by Susan's. I found several imprints of men's shoes in the carpet. They look like size 11 and ½. I can't be sure they were all from the same person, but based on the travel pattern you told me, I found some going to the bedroom and then out to the kitchen. Her place was trashed, but I am not sure they knew what they were looking for because they went through everything. I think we should go back there and lock the door with the key. This wasn't a forced entry."

I unlocked the door bolt when I went to check out Susan's place, leaving it open for black shoes to come right in. I remembered that I had Susan's diary from the visit, but kept that quiet. Mitch left.

The kids and I took Matt for his walk. I knew Steve was worried because Steve doesn't do family walks in the neighborhood with the dog even after Thanksgiving dinner. They stayed with me and we watched movies until Max got home. I love my family.

Max was notably concerned, hugging me and holding on for several minutes. The issue was that life keeps happening even after a car bomb. We had no distinct plan that would guarantee my safety. We were finally taking events seriously; the bomb linked the threat and danger to me. I know Max felt helpless, but I absolutely did not want him feeling responsible for my life, literally. We still believed I was taking all the necessary precautions, but this bomb sure took us by surprise!

TWENTY-TWO

I DECIDED NOT to go to work on Monday because I could just see the police report section in the local paper – Claudia Monroe's car blown up at the shooting range. Max and I slept in, meaning 8 o'clock. We cooked blueberry pancakes, sausage links, and scrambled eggs. Every week I make a run to Costco because they stock the best fruit like blueberries, blackberries, strawberries, pears, apples, and grapes even when they are not in season. Blueberry pancakes are a tradition for special occasions in our family. Marissa and I ate blueberry pancakes when I visited her at college. Max and I eat blueberry pancakes for breakfast when we go fishing. Now we eat them after car bombs.

Detective Andrews arrived at the house to give us a summary of the evidence that was collected.

"The bomb appeared to be attached to the bottom of your car with a pressure trigger to set off the detonator. When you started to sit down, the bomb was triggered. The fact that you jumped out and ran to grab the guns and ammo saved your life. The bomb looked professionally made, and was attached to your car at some point during your target practice with Steve.

As for Susan's condo, a crime scene team was not able to get fingerprints from whoever trashed it. No unaccountable prints were found including in the letter picked up from Susan's mom. The handwriting did not match the printing of the letter that came to the gym, although the postmark was MidTown too."

We silently waited for more information.

He continued. "Someone must not want you digging into Susan's stuff. What do you know or have that they want? Or what don't they want you to tell or find? After the bombing, I would have to say that at least Susan's death and the threats toward you must be connected. I'm not sure if Mick's death is related to you or if it is related to the embezzlement scheme or if somehow Susan is tied into that too. 'They,' the bad guys, must think you know something or will find something."

"I don't know what that would be and can't even begin to imagine what my involvement is."

Later that day, I called Susan's mom telling her the results of the letter. I told her that someone had gone to Susan's condo and torn it apart, but volunteered to make sure it was cleaned up.

"If the police are through investigating her apartment, I suppose I should sell it. I'm just not ready yet. Some evidence might still be there that is related to her death. If you could arrange for it to be cleaned up, that would be great. Let me know if anything is destroyed or ruined," she said.

I'm thinking the only thing I've done lately is to go through Susan's condo and almost get caught. Maybe black shoes did know I was in there or someone saw me leave. Whatever I was almost blown up for must have to do with my visit. Being blown up is a bigger statement than, say, the competition slashing prices to take my members away.

TWENTY-THREE

TUESDAY IS BACK to business. Max drove me to work before returning to his installation project in Tennessee. I insisted that hanging around with me would not be helpful, but would make me feel like he was hovering.

I decided not to create a mass emailing of 5,000 people, most of whom would not welcome the intrusion. Starting with my own network, Marissa was going to make a list from my email account, Facebook friends, and LinkedIn acquaintances. These people were going to be my main line of communication. Hopefully, they would pass my email along to people they thought would be interested in fitness or personal training. People that I know or have met are more likely to put in a good word for me than strangers receiving unsolicited emails.

The air smelled like chocolate when Charlene walked in to the building. She was consuming chocolate covered donut holes, creating very sticky fingers. When Bob arrived, the three of us talked about the circumstances that surrounded us. We considered a variety of answers or reasons for all the dubious activity. None of us had any brilliant light bulb ideas, and speculation is sometimes more of a problem than a solution. I asked Bob to close up that night so Charlene and I could clean Susan's condo.

"Wait a minute!" said Charlene. "Don't I get a choice in this? I don't ever mind helping out, but this is the place that you were almost nabbed by black shoes, and may have gotten blown up for visiting."

"We'll lock the door, Charlene."

That was laughable.

"Now just a reminder to myself and you both," I said. "We are here to run a business even though a lot of crazy and upsetting events keep taking our attention away. Bob, you and I have to focus. When we are with clients, that time is their time and they have our full attention. We are not going to let outside circumstances get in the way of great customer service."

"That's a lecture, not a reminder," said Bob. I suppose it was.

Helen came in for a training session with me. I enjoyed working with her because she was into challenges and was upbeat about life. Her red hair was gorgeous as always, thick and framing her face even though she pulled it back to workout. We did a lot of lunges with rotation, worked lower body with the cables, and upper body with the TRX. She was looking good and lifting strong. She explained that her career focused on being the liaison between a real estate company and a mortgage lending company. She could get customers pre-qualified and then qualified to finance real estate purchases made through her firm. It sounded like an interesting job and she definitely had the communication skills to be successful.

A little later Sam came in to train. He wanted to talk. He wanted to talk about me not him. I reminded him that this was his time and we needed to concentrate on his training needs.

"If this is the only time I can spend with you, then we need make it more than just lifting."

"Sam, this isn't about me. It's about you."

"I know. I need to know you are okay. I want to somehow help all this chaos in your life go away." He smiled slightly.

"Sam, I have no answers. Right now life is better just trying to stick to running a business."

I pushed him on biceps, triceps, and chest. He definitely needed me to spot him before we were through.

Becca came into the gym for the first time since her injury. Her doctor gave her clearance to do specific lower body strength exercises on the machines. She wore a neon pink cast on her right arm up to her elbow. Wow. She spoke to whomever she knew and answered questions they asked. Neon pink is hard to miss. Eventually, she went to work on the hamstring and quad machines. She could do squats and lunges with no resistance because she wasn't ready to have weight in her hands or on her shoulders. Lucky her balance is good.

Late in the day, Charlene and I left the gym, leaving Bob in charge. Charlene drove to Susan's and would drive me home afterward. We parked close to the concrete stairs that went up to her condo. I checked #3C mail again. Nothing. As we walked to her condo, I realized the door was still unlocked because I left in such a hurry the other day. On TV the good guys go around with a gun and check each room to make sure there are no bad guys hiding out. We kind of did that first, then we locked ourselves in and shut the blinds.

"Wow, this place is a mess," Charlene said.

"As we are picking up, check everything and make sure you know what its purpose is. If we don't know what something is for, let's keep it until we find out," I said.

We worked methodically, straightening up furniture, stacking papers, putting pillows back on the furniture, and throwing away trash. We looked at books, journals, and magazines. We put clothes and shoes away in the closet and drawers. We picked up her scattered toiletry articles and threw them away. No need for those now. We worked silently.

"I think I can feel her spirit," said Charlene.

"Maybe you can," I said. "It's kind of hard not to have feelings since we are going through all of her things."

I put the pictures back in their frames.

"I'm going back in the living room to finish looking through those books and put them back on the shelves," Charlene said.

"I'll go to the kitchen next," I said.

Some of the dishes were broken, so I swept up the glass and threw it away. I had already cleaned out the refrigerator. A few cookbooks looked like they had been flung off the shelves. After flipping through the pages, I stacked them back on the shelf. Something in the Betty Crocker cookbook caught my eye. I flipped through it again and saw a newspaper clipping folded up between the pages. There were actually two newspaper articles, one from Atlanta, Georgia, and one from Charlotte, North Carolina. Who reads a hard copy of the newspaper any more? How did she get copies from Atlanta and Charlotte? They were both about a real estate company called Southern Life. They were both dated in September this year. There's that real estate theme again. I put them in the pile of items we were saving to take with us.

Charlene found a notepad with Susan's notes for training exercises for her clients. To illustrate an exercise, we all draw these stick figures of people in different positions to represent exercises that we want to remember to do. That way the drawings remind us the correct form and movement for an exercise. The pictures look a little silly, but are fairly effective.

When we were through, Susan's condo was in order and organized. We vacuumed, put some Mr. Clean in the toilet bowl and got ready to leave. We turned out all the lights then looked out the windows to see if anyone was visible. Together we went out the door, locked it, and walked straight to Charlene's car. I dropped to the ground and looked underneath the vehicle for a bomb. The bottom of the car looked okay, but what do I know? We got in, and Charlene drove me home.

I made sure I knew where the gun and ammunition were before I went to bed. No walk for Matt tonight. He followed me relentlessly, begging me to take him. Sorry, boy, not tonight.

TWENTY-FOUR

MARISSA PICKED ME up and drove me to work. Halloween was Sunday. Four more days. We put a plastic pumpkin out at the gym with small treats inside. Reactions were amazing. Some people take the treats and put them in their pockets or mouths and some people complain that we would even consider putting treats out at a gym. We're just being hospitable and going with the culture of the area. ☺

I called Joe, our terrific Internet guru, and asked him to look up the dates and times that the negative web messages were entered about OverTheTop and me. He said he would email them. I asked him to email the IP address of the computer that was used as well.

Members were chatting as they arrived for the morning cardio class. We were also trying a different class format today. I was conducting a group TRX class. TRX is a form of suspension training using your own body weight and your positioning as the resistance. This is for strength and core, but can get very cardio too. Canvas type straps are suspended from overhead at an anchor point or hook. The straps have handle bars and foot stirrups. A sign advertised a free TRX class with ten openings. We hung ten TRX anchors and attached the straps with the carabiners.

When you are just starting out on the TRX, it feels a little uncoordinated and clumsy; suspension training gets more graceful as you practice. After a brief description and demonstration of the TRX, the group started exercises. We did standing exercises like the sprinter start, squat and lunge, standing upper body exercises like the row, chest press, triceps, and biceps. Exercises on the ground included planks, abs, hamstrings and bridges. After 30 minutes, everyone was ready for a stretch. I may just add this class to the schedule. I'd call the trial a success.

Bob was taking the day off. Thankfully, there were no trivia questions today. Marissa was in the office working on my email list and the client database. Charlene welcomed members at the front counter.

Mitch appeared. "Well, the biggest mistake they made so far was not killing you because now we know you are a target."

"Thanks," I said.

OverTheTop

"Here's one for you. Bill Moody is really Harold Moore who works for a company called The Rental Company that is a subsidiary of the corporation Real Estate Ventures. I haven't figured out his role here yet, but he is involved with the whole real estate theme going around. Was he here to keep tabs on Mick or to kill him? Is he a good guy here to uncover the truth? His title is officially financial advisor. How generic can you get? And why does he seem so interested in Susan?"

I replied, "I suggest we just live life like we don't know any different. Bob and I and all of us will be wary around him and make sure we are not alone with him. Maybe he will say or do something that gives us more information about his mission," I said.

Changing the subject, I asked her if she could do anything about getting a copy of the video from the college's computer lab on the day the Internet was used to tarnish my reputation?

"That would be Monday the 18th sometime between 8 and 10 AM."

"I can try, if not I'll talk to Andrews to get a little official push behind it," Mitch said. And she was gone.

I called over to Charlene and asked her to come by me.

"Charlene, we need to get into Mick's house."

"What?" she asked.

"Oh you heard me. We need to look around to see if there is anything that connects him to Susan. The police just hem and hah over the connection. They've had their chance to look."

"Why are you including me in all of your adventures, now? Are we bringing a gun? How are we getting in? Unlocking the door?"

"You can figure out anything with the Internet, even picking a lock. Steve can solve the rubiks cube every time just by following instructions he gets on the web. Besides, I can ask Mitch. Also, you know I could never get away with going to Mick's house if Max were in town."

"True. Don't you think the police would have found a connection?" asked Charlene.

"The police first thought his death was a suicide. Then they knew it was a murder. They were looking for a murderer. Even now they don't connect Susan with Mick's death. We have to find out what happened. I'm the alive person involved now." I was quiet for a moment.

"Okay, so let's do a few slow drive-bys during lunch to see if we can figure out what type of locks are on the house and where the doors are. I'm not sure what to do if there is an alarm system that is turned on. Run fast, I guess. We are experienced at running away fast. We can see if there is any activity or if the police tape is down. A whole week has passed, and the police should have collected any evidence they needed. They just released the body. I doubt anyone is cleaning out his personal things this soon after his death."

Marissa was running the gym during lunch hour. We got in Charlene's car.

"Let's drive around several blocks in different directions to see if we can tell if someone is following us. Like on TV," I said.

We finally got to Mick's house. The police tape was still up in front of the door. Seeing the house gave me a good mental layout of the building in my head. Turning the car around in the next block, we drove by in the other direction. There must be an entrance from the garage into the house, and back doors too. I didn't see deadlocks.

We returned to the gym. In the quiet part of the afternoon, I called Mitch and asked about picking a lock.

"Don't you do it. I'm not sure where you are breaking into, but it's not worth it."

She told me how to pick a lock anyway and how to use a credit card depending on the type of the lock. I also found all of this information during a search on the Internet.

Charlene and I made plans to go to Mick's the next morning. I asked Bob if he would open the gym. Charlene would drive. We were going to circle around to avoid being followed and try getting in the house by the door in back. We decided to go in when we would be least expected – early in the morning.

Marissa drove me home from work. Max will be back Friday night, and I will be glad to see him. In the meantime, I have a business and an investigation to run.

I practiced picking a lock using a tension wrench and a couple of paper clips. Matt just watched, wondering what I was trying to accomplish. I also tried using a credit card to slide open the lock. That touch needed to be a little more sensitive than it looks on TV.

TWENTY-FIVE

WE WERE UNDER the cover of darkness when Charlene picked me up. My gun was in the case and the ammunition in my purse. We were both dressed in black although I don't know what good black will be when the sun comes up. We circled around several streets and parked on the block behind Mick's house. As we approached the back door, Mitch appeared. She put her finger to her lips to say, "Shh."

A window on the side panel of the back door was already broken. So much for all the practice trying to pick a lock! I pulled out the cleaning gloves I brought from the gym, and we all put on a pair. Reaching through the broken window I unlocked the door. I loaded my gun as Mitch pulled a gun out from behind her back. We all huddled together and she slowly pushed the door open.

Mick's house was a mess just like Susan's. You would think that if a place was still a crime scene, the police would have someone monitoring it. The sky was getting brighter making the inside of the house visible. We went from room to room checking to be sure that we were alone.

"Charlene, you check the kitchen. Mitch, will you take the master bedroom and bathroom? I will look in his office. Remember we are not cleaning up, we're just trying to find some connection between all these crimes. Thirty minutes max, and then we're out of here," I said.

We all went quietly to our assignments and began to sift through the papers and items thrown about on the floor. I knew the police would have collected a lot of evidence, but we still may find something that makes sense to us. Getting a feel for Mick's surroundings added to the picture we were trying to put together.

Mick was divorced and had two grown children, both in their twenties, both living in apartments just outside of town. I assumed they would be handling the arrangements for his service. I wondered how they felt about the embezzlement allegations against their father. I believed they were very upset about his death.

I searched about half way through the room when I noticed Mick kept a fitness journal. He recorded when he worked out, what activity he did, and what muscles he used. I put the book in the pile to take with us. Some members or clients keep journals as a form of motivation and as a way to measure progress.

We didn't find any more information, but being able to visualize the scene helped me develop a mental picture of the crime. We left through the back door and followed Mitch to her car. After she drove us to Charlene's car, I bent down and looked under the car. What a bomb looks like I don't know, but I had to check.

What we have here is murder and mayhem. Murder and mayhem.

Charlene and I circled a few blocks and drove to the gym via the local bakery for chocolate covered cream puffs.

"What is the Mona Lisa missing?" Bob asked as we walked in the door.

"Dunno," I said.

"Her eyebrows," Bob said.

"Huh," I said. Trivia got annoying after a while.

I was reviewing what was on the schedule for Thursday (today) when Bob said, "Mick's memorial service has been set for Saturday at 10 AM. Are we going?"

"I don't think we should close the gym, so unless you or Charlene feel some close personal ties to Mick, I will go and represent OverTheTop."

Mitch appeared. She had a copy of the video of the college computer lab during the times the IP address was used. Bob, Mitch, and I watched the video on my computer. I saw nothing meaningful.

"Wait. I think that's a trainer from PowerUp," Bob said.

The trainer was the only person using the computer during the timeframe we knew the comments were sent out.

"This is getting curiouser and curiouser," I said.

We went to the PowerUp website and scanned for personal trainers. Sure enough, this guy's picture was on the webpage. His name was Todd Horne. He was in his early twenties with a medium build and curly brown hair.

"How would you like the last name Horne?" I asked.

No one answered.

I wasn't sure what to do with this information except file it with all the other input we collected. I wasn't ready to press charges just yet. I needed to know more about what the whole picture looked like. I wanted to know what was going on around here!

Max called, and I made sure I was alone because I never like people hearing my phone conversations. He wanted reassurance that nothing crazy was happening. I assured him that all was well. I told him that I missed him and was looking forward to tomorrow night. He knew what I meant. Usually after Max has been out of town, we have great sex and enjoy sleeping together again. We decided to go car shopping this weekend after he comes home too. I may just get a 4WD Rav4 Toyota this time.

OverTheTop

Late in the afternoon, Detective Andrews came into my office. My insides were shaking because he couldn't find out that we were in Mick's house, and I didn't know if I made a good liar or not. I had the feeling I would get plenty of practice not being truthful before all the mysteries ended. I'm not directly lying, just withholding truth. Which is really lying itself and is against my principles and the principles of living yoga off the mat.

"Mick's place was messed up just like Susan's," Andrews said.

"Huh," I said.

"That makes a connection between the two murders as far as I'm concerned," he said. "We're going to sift through all the evidence again trying to look at it from a different angle."

"That's good to know. Makes me feel better. Finally have a direction to look in."

"I understand you got a copy of the computer lab video." This wasn't a question. His perturbed manner showed me he wasn't happy.

"I just had the idea and thought we could find out who made the negative Internet comments."

"Gathering evidence is my job," he said.

"Then I'm sure you will want a copy."

"What did you find?"

"One of my trainers recognized a trainer from PowerUp using the computer. We looked him up on their website. His name is Todd Horne."

He asked, "How would you like a last name like Horne?"

I didn't answer.

"I'm going to bring him in for questioning."

When I got home, Matt followed me around the house waiting for his walk. I finally got frustrated at him and decided to take him out to make him happy and stop him from hounding me. When he wants to take a walk he will follow me from room to room to room until I give up. He's a runner and loves to runaway so I use two collars hooked to his leash when we walk.

I was very mindful of our surroundings, and we stuck close to home. He was happy to be out. We were never out of site of at least one of our neighbors' homes, not that I felt comfortable going to any of them for help.

I fed Matt a combination of dry dog food mixed with a little warm water and a couple of tablespoons of canned food when we got home. I didn't feel like spending time cooking for myself so I ate left over beef barley soup with whole grain bread.

After dinner, I settled down on the couch with Mick's fitness journal, Susan's diary, and the newspaper clippings trying to research the items and find a connection between the crimes.

I would consider Mick a well-seasoned fitness buff. In other words, physical activity and working out were a permanent part of his lifestyle. This was something he had been doing for a long time.

Reading his journal was interesting because he really paid attention to his progress and how he was feeling each day. Some days a person might not feel so energetic or might feel off his game and that would affect the quality of a workout. Mick's goals were specific and measureable, such as, increase bicep resistance by 10 pounds within 6 weeks while continuing to do 3 sets of 10 reps.

I also noticed that he used 'technical' terms, like anterior delts and glutes. Often times with new clients, I encourage them to put an exercise in their own words when making an exercise log. For instance, when I was teaching a client about squats for the first time, she wrote down 'chair' and 'sit back.' This helps remind them of first, what the exercise is, and second, what good form is. Mick was way past that. He had his terminology down.

I did not have a record of what Mick did before I started running OverTheTop. This journal began when OverTheTop started and he was training with Susan. He mentioned her several times when he referred to her advice or to information she had given him. He always wrote down the date and time of his workouts and his training sessions. As I got toward the end of the journal, I noticed three different days and times that he was meeting with Susan, but he did not record what muscle groups he worked. That seemed unusual, but we all get busy sometimes and don't always finish things the way we want. Similar to keeping a food journal, sometimes you just don't get around to writing down what you put in your mouth by the end of the day.

I put Mick's journal down and started reading Susan's diary. I felt like I was intruding on someone's private life, and I was. Just because Susan wasn't alive anymore didn't mean that her thoughts, feelings, and memories weren't valuable or meaningful. Sometimes I read too much information about how a date ended up or about a disagreement between friends. So far I found nothing relevant to work or Mick.

I let Matt outside one last time to use the bathroom and crawled into bed. I fell asleep wondering if this was her first diary ever or where her other ones were kept.

OverTheTop

TWENTY-SIX

FRIDAY MORNINGS ARE always busy at the gym with Zumba, Becca's hi/lo class now being subbed by Kathy, and strength. I knew that Bill Moody aka Harold Moore was scheduled to train with Bob. That was a little nerve wracking. I also had Helen on my agenda for the day, and Friday is a Sam Good day.

I wanted to double check with Susan's previous clients to make sure they were placed with trainers that met their needs and were available during the times when the client wanted to schedule. I took the trainers schedules and mapped appointments against the master calendar. Something was bothering me, like I wasn't making all the connections between trainers and clients. I would need to finish another time because I didn't know what I was missing.

I went upstairs to check on the boxing equipment because a client was coming in for training. As I stepped into the stairwell, I just had this funny feeling that something pokey had been going on in there. Maybe it was a slight odor or maybe I was just having strange out of mind experiences today.

I returned to the counter as Bob came up and said, "It wasn't me this time."

"Oh, yeah? What do you know about the current stairwell action?" I asked.

"Nothing. Hey, how many pounds of lipstick does a woman eat in her lifetime?"

"Dunno."

"Six pounds."

"Gross." Bob and his trivia.

I looked at him and said, "Let's plan our strategy for when Bill comes into workout."

"Unless I literally call him by his other name, how will he know that I know he isn't who he says he is?" Bob asked.

"Just react the way you always have when he brings up Susan, cautiously and generally. Let me know how it goes."

"Gottcha."

Later as I was working with Helen, I noticed Bill Moody walk through the gym to meet with Bob in a multi-purpose room. I crossed my fingers, but this was Helen's training time so I was focused on her. We were doing some Pilates with props to continue to strengthen her core. Foam rollers and the Bosu are good for core strengthening exercises. The Pilates mat series is also excellent for core stability, back to basics and difficult at the same time.

I asked Helen how the economy was affecting local real estate prices. She thought housing in our area was losing value, but not at a high rate like other areas of the country. She suggested that the downturn in the economy opened up a lot of room for scammers to come up with schemes to cheat people. One example she gave me was short-term companies would 're-finance' mortgages, but would scam the funds because a mortgage would not really exist. Our conversation was intermittent as we concentrated on her breathing for core exercises. Helen has strong abs, and her progress is amazing.

Later, Rachel was scheduled to train me in my self-defense maneuvers. She spent time telling me how to avoid attacks, like being aware of your surroundings at all times. Plan what to do if you were attacked in your car or in a home invasion. Decide how to protect your home or have a safe room in your house. Avoid isolated locations or dark places. Travel with someone else. There is safety in numbers. Consider other defense mechanisms such as pepper spray, tasers, stun guns, and batons. Walk or jog on a variety of courses. Carry your cell phone with you.

Rachel is about my height. She has short dark hair and wears loose baggy pants. Her dad was a boxer and she danced. Putting her experiences all together, she became an advisor on self-defense techniques.

Rachel lifts so she is strong and muscular in a feminine way. Women don't usually bulk up the way men do. Hormones, right?

Now along came Sam. We worked together in a conversational manner talking about his reps and sets, how much weight he uses for each exercise, and his progress. We have an easy relationship, just naturally connecting with each other's thoughts and ideas. We're in agreement on many of those ideas. There's just that awkward pull or attraction that developed as we spent more time training together. He is someone who is good to look at and touch, I'll say that.

Back at the front desk, Mitch appeared as if from nowhere. She was just here. "Andrews interviewed Todd Horne, and Horne says his boss, Charles Johnson, gave him $100 to go to that computer lab and enter the Internet comments about you. Charles Johnson denies all knowledge of the situation and fired Todd."

"That Charles Johnson from PowerUp just seems to keep coming up again and again. Can you find out his address? I want to drive by his house to get a feel about what kind of person he is besides a jerk," I asked.

"Got it. 123 Whitetail Street. That's over in the Caldwell Woods subdivision. Remember this isn't personal."

I said thanks, but she was already gone.

OverTheTop

Charlene was driving me home from work so we did the drive by Charles' house together. The neighborhood was a typical MidTown neighborhood. Many of the houses had the same architecture, probably four bedrooms, two and a half baths, and double car garage. His lawn was well kept. He seemed to fit right in with the rest of the area, although, you never know who is a sleazebag behind closed doors.

Max was home when Charlene dropped me off.

"How was your week?" he asked.

"Great, you?"

We were home alone together for a change. No time for dinner. No time for conversation. We headed straight upstairs and got frisky. Yum, yum. Spooning through the night made me feel safe and secure regardless of life outside our home.

Matt slept in the family room.

Nancy Klotz

TWENTY-SEVEN

SATURDAY MORNING I drove Max's car to the memorial service for Mick. Ironically, his service took place in the same United Church of Christ that Susan was in a few weeks earlier. The burgundy pews were polished to a shiny gloss. Each row was filling in with mourners, and I sat closer to the back in an aisle seat. Mick's son and one of Mick's partners from his realty company both spoke to eulogize his life. When the minister completed the last prayer, I exited the church taking one of the orange FUNERAL signs for the car from the funeral attendant.

A funeral procession is always interesting to me because I like the way other cars pull over to let you pass. The cemetery was just blocks from the church, the cars all lined up in the cemetery driveway as the passengers gathered around the gravesite. I recognized Bill Moody as one of the mourners. He was in a gray suit with a blue shirt and a striped tie. He was alone; his sorrowful demeanor seemed sincere. The service at the site was short and seemed surreal to me to think that Mick's body was in the casket that was being lowered into the ground. Even though we trained together just a few times, I felt like we knew each other. Now he's gone.

As I watched the ceremony, a movement caught my eye across the way from behind a large oak tree in the next block of the cemetery. I was not sure I actually saw someone until a head looked around the tree. Dressed in a brown coat with a scarf covering his face and a brown hat on his head, a man pointed his index finger and thumb in the shape of a gun and pulled the trigger on me. I moved away from the group and ran towards the tree. A gray sedan was pulling out of the cemetery on to the road, but I couldn't get the plates. The man was nowhere in sight so I assumed he had driven away. Whether he was alone or not, I couldn't tell.

What the heck was that all about? Was that a threat, warning, or a prophecy?

Steve was meeting me at the target range after the service. I was practicing with both the Ruger and the Sig. The SR9 Ruger was for the house. The Sig is what I carry with me on our adventures. I was getting better with my aim. The laser sight sure helped for shorter distances, although it bounced around when I tried to sight on a target. The bouncing red dot reminds me of how unsteady my hand can be.

Steve has a Bushmaster AR-15 rifle. I can hardly believe that: An assault gun in MidTown. That gun is actually illegal in the next county. He enjoys target practice on the outdoor ranges though. Sometimes target practice is limited by how much he can afford to spend on ammunition. He likes moving targets. I bet my target will be moving when I actually need to shoot someone.

I'm so ready to use my guns. Give me a reason.

Steve and I both stooped on hands and knees to take a look under the car for a bomb before I got in to drive away.

On the drive back home, I took a detour to see where Bill Moody was living. The buildings looked clean and were white cinder block covered with stucco. The apartments could be compared to hotel rooms for short term or temporary housing. I am sure they came equipped with a sitting room and some sort of appliances for the kitchen. I didn't see his car in the lot and continued to drive home.

Max and I grilled fish even though it was cold outside. After dinner we made our way to the Toyota dealer to check out the Rav4 cars on the lot. Here's Max's strategy. Sales people and sales administration are really ready to go home on a Saturday night so they are less likely to spend hours wanting to negotiate. They just want the deal to be done so they can get out of there.

OverTheTop

I bought a pretty blue, 6 cylinder, 4 wheel drive Rav4 with black and gray leather interior and needed practice with the automatic keys. This car has some pep and picks up speed in an instant. The gas pedal is real sensitive. ☺

The next morning we woke up to celebrate Sunday and Halloween. This year the holiday is a big deal in MidTown. "Society" has declared the day to be costume day. People dress up and walk the shops and restaurants downtown. Several years ago, the town declared a Harry Potter Day to celebrate one of the new books coming out. You could see people in witch hats and capes through out the day. Max and I went for a walk downtown and bought two coffees. We saw a wide variety of interesting people in costumes: witches, jesters, pirates, and Ursula the octopus. Only in America, right?

Later in the day Max settled in to finish some quotes he needed to complete for work. I returned to Susan's diary. Finally something. In one of the entries closer to the end of her life, she wrote – "Mick – Southern Life." Now where had I heard of that name before? I went through the stack of items we brought out of both places. There were the two newspaper articles that fell out of Susan's cookbook. Neither article seemed to have any important information other than purchases the company recently made. Hmm… I read the rest of her diary, but didn't pull out any more clues. I was going to ask Mitch and Joe to research Southern Life and see if there was any relevance to Susan or the real estate scam.

I worked on designing a new membership drive for OverTheTop. We were having special offers in November and December to try to increase our membership numbers. The new membership specials were going to be a choice of 1) no enrollment fee 2) one month free membership or 3) a free six-week special mind/body class when joining the gym. Then I needed to create specials for current members to purchase as holiday gifts before Christmas. We would offer personal training packages at a discounted rate. We could also offer a package of guest passes for a discounted price. Some guests might eventually become members. I needed to work out the details and logistics, but that would be for another day.

After the trick-or-treaters were gone and before I crawled into bed with Max, my cell phone rang. Uh-oh, that was rarely good. Mitch was calling to tell me that she had been watching Bill Moody's activities. Interestingly enough, she ran across him on what looked like a Saturday night date. He was out at Harry's with none other than Helen, my client. Harry's was a hopping restaurant/bar in downtown MidTown with great martinis. They certainly weren't trying to hide anything if they were at a well known and popular place. I was definitely gonna need sex with Max to put that one out of my mind for the night.

TWENTY-EIGHT

MONDAY MORNING AT OverTheTop, Charlene was that excited kind of excited when you can hardly contain yourself. She was definitely glowing and bursting at the seams. She bounced around full of energy checking in clients and members and filing membership cards when handing out locker keys. When we were alone for a few minutes, I asked her what was up.

"OMG! Sam Good is the owner and chief executive officer of KYX Manufacturing Company. He definitely is made of the bucks and used to be married to that actress who ended up partying too much and ruining her career. Her name's Amanda and she's naturally got that kind of long wavy hair that some women spend tons of money on at the salon for the same effect. She was the one playing the manipulative vixen in the Hill Top soap opera. After the divorce, her partying turned to drugs and her appearance went downhill. Or maybe the divorce came after the drugs. They got divorced three years ago and thankfully do not have any kids. He is single! And we know where he works out!!!"

"Charlene, what have you done?" I asked.

"All's you have to do is Google him. He comes up all over the Internet. There are all sorts of articles about his company, his ex-wife, his home, and his money. Why didn't you tell me we had a celebrity training here?"

"Charlene, I didn't know. It's none of our business. He's a client, although he does seem to have an interesting life, now that you mention it. Hmmm! Did you find out anything else?"

"Here, look. He has a dog, a golden lab. Here's a picture of Sam throwing a stick to the dog on the front lawn of his company. His dog's name is Rover. How original. His company made over 30 million dollars last year alone! His marketing campaign has shoved KYX up above the competition. You could learn something from him."

"Geez, Charlene, how am I supposed to act like I don't know any of this next time he comes in. It's almost like stalking him," I said. "He comes in tomorrow for training, much less several days a week to work out."

"Why don't you ask him what he does for a living, or where he lives, or something personal?" Charlene suggested.

"He doesn't need any encouragement!" I said.

Tiger Lady walked in through the doorway with her little ponytail pulled through her little ball cap. She looked all ready for an audience. She does have her following. When she originally came in with a neon pink cast, half the female members came in later that week in neon pink clothes. Some people have actually asked me to call them when she was having a sub, so they wouldn't have to waste their time coming to class. Then again, some people have been seen on the treadmill during her class because they didn't feel like 'being lectured.' It just goes to show you, to each her own!

"A little over 5 weeks till I get my cast off," she said as she brushed past us into the weight area. "Still doing my modified workout!"

I looked at Charlene and said, "I want to say, 'How did we get so lucky?' but I suppose with her popularity, we really are lucky to have her working here even though it doesn't feel like she's a real catch."

I began working on my own training schedule. With life being so busy, I fell behind in my workouts and felt like my time was spread so thin that I couldn't meet all my needs. I jog, swim, lift, and do defensive training with Rachel, yoga, Pilates, and TRX. I made a calendar for the next month trying to schedule all my workouts in even if they were on a limited basis. Three days to jog, two days to strength train, at least one day to swim (although that is pathetic), four yoga classes a week in addition to a short practice at home each day, Pilates twice, and Rachel when she could come train me to defend myself. I also needed to add in target practice. Wow! Creating workout combinations for each day and trying to achieve all my training requirements was overwhelming.

I am fit, but sometimes am quite humbled at how weak or 'not strong' I am. Depending on the activity, sometimes I feel weak, like doing pull-ups, pushups, opening certain jar lids, unscrewing tight knobs, and lifting heavy objects.

I reviewed Susan's training schedule again and needed to put together any ideas I could find from her training journal and Mick's work out notes. I wondered if any of Susan's neighbors had seen her with anyone in particular. And what about Mick?

Max was working late on a project that needed to be shipped by the end of the week. That evening I curled up in a stuffed leather chair taking a much needed break and read one of my favorite author's murder mystery books. I was happy to be driving my new car to and from work. I felt like the craziness was dying down a little even though there were so many unanswered questions. I used the time to forget and act like life was normal.

TWENTY-NINE

MAX GOT UP early and left for work. He likes to set the alarm really early then press snooze for an hour as it goes off every ten minutes. I hate that. I always wake up when the alarm first goes off and stay awake for the hour, losing sixty minutes of sleep. The noise the alarm makes is just plain old annoying. Before I got out of bed, I remembered to be thankful for a new day and stretched my hips and back. My cell phone rang. Uh-oh. That is never good news.

When I answered, a nurse from our local hospital, MidTown General was talking fast and low, and said, "I don't know if I should be calling you or not, but he keeps asking for you, although the police are still here and don't want anyone coming by."

"What in the world are you talking about?" I asked.

"Sam. Sam Good. He's here. A bullet in the back. Not in great shape, but still hanging in there."

"What happened?"

"He has blunt trauma to the back of his head and a bullet wound in his back. Thankfully it missed major organs and arteries. He's in and out, but he wants you. His good physical condition is definitely a plus."

"I'll be right there."

"He's out of emergency and surgery and in the ICU. My name is Melinda. If you come up to the third floor, I can show you what room he's in and see if the police will let you visit. He doesn't seem to have any other family nearby."

I could feel my blood pumping hard through my veins. I heard each heart beat in my head and knew I was close to shear panic. I rushed around to get dressed and let Matt out. What else did I need to think of before I left the house? I slowed down and focused on my yoga breathing. Grabbing my purse and cell phone, I drove my car over to the hospital.

Maneuvering the parking deck at the hospital is always a challenge and today was no better. I drove around each corner hoping to find an empty space. Finally, I parked and made my way to the elevators going to the third floor. The hospital was always so busy with people going to ER, out patient services, or visiting friends and family, that no one noticed me at all.

Sam's room was in a newer part of the building. When the elevator opened on the third floor, I could tell who Melinda was immediately. She was tall and big busted, a solid large build, but not fat. Definitely a woman used to being in charge. She spotted me right away too and motioned for me to come by her. As we walked down the dimly lit hallway, who else did we see, but, Detective Andrews, of course.

"You might as well go in, he says your name occasionally. See if you can get him to say anything about what happened."

I pushed the door open to room 313 and walked towards the bed. All the linens were white, so were the walls. The sterile room dramatized the seriousness of Sam's injuries. I could see Sam's shape under the sheets. He still seemed built, but somehow deflated and very pale. His eyes opened a little as I approached and he made a small movement with his hand. I took his hand in mine and sat there in silence with him as he drifted off somewhere.

Melinda came in and checked the monitors that were hooked to the tubes and cords attached to Sam's body. Her fiddling and diddling became obvious as she said, "Pain meds are very important to keep patients calm and comfortable. Sometimes they also keep a person from waking up enough to talk. Let's just see…"

"Why are you so interested?" I asked.

"Because this is one good looking man. There is no reason for a man looking as nice as that to be shot. This wasn't an accident. Sometimes you help the innocent victims out."

"I hear you on that," I replied.

"He has a sister coming in from Virginia. She won't be here until later." Melinda left the room.

The MidTown hospital had recently been renovated. All patients' rooms were private. Sam's room looked ultra modern with a one step curved tray ceiling that added an artistic element. There was a set of recessed lights in the ceiling and another in the dropped step of the ceiling. Seemed like quite an upgrade for a hospital room. There was an alcove with a window and a built-in couch that converted to a bed that didn't look very comfortable.

My thoughts wandered to everything that happened in the last month as I sat quietly while Sam slept. Trying to keep the business going, Susan's death, the vandalism, the cat, the letters, the Internet, PowerUp's ads, Mick's death, the car blowing up, and now Sam. What? Is there a black mark following me around? And here I thought you could make your own positive energy each day by being positive?

"You're here," I heard Sam say. We smiled at each other.

"I think this is all about you," he said slowly and quietly. "You need to be careful. Think of all the things that have happened in your life recently. I want to help you find out what is going on."

"What happened?" I asked.

"I'm not sure. I heard a noise outside that sounded like a thud or something big being dropped. I looked out the window and someone came up from behind. They must have been in the house knowing the noise would distract me. Something bashed my head when I looked for the distraction outside. Then there was a lot of heat in my back. What did happen?"

"Well, all's I know is that you were hit on the back of your head with something. I don't know what yet. You have a bullet wound in your back. You mentioned my name a few times. And your sister is coming in from Virginia."

"Wow. No wonder my head aches and my back feels like it's been sliced in half."

"You rest now. I will be coming in to check on you."

"Claudia, please. Don't let my ex, Amanda, near me," Sam said as he fell into a drugged sleep.

I left the room and found Melinda at the nurse's station. The computers and monitors were flashing like a command control center.

"We have a mission. We ladies need to unite. We can't let Sam's ex, Amanda, near him. I promised. She's that actress from here that was in the Hill Top soap opera, but partied herself out on drugs and booze last year."

"Will do. I'll tell the other nurses at the station that she is not welcome."

Detective Andrews was waiting for me down the hall.

"Sam said he heard something outside and when he looked, he was hit from behind. For some reason, he thinks this has to do with me. I'm going to be losing friends fast if they all end up shot or dead. Are you protecting him since he is still alive? Someone might come in to finish him off. I've seen it on TV."

"We'll watch after him. I'll let you know when we find out something."

I went back to the elevators and walked my way back to the car in the parking garage. Slowly backing out, I noticed a black escalade SUV tearing around the upper corner of the deck, smashing against the rear end of the car on the corner, heading straight for me. Punching the accelerator, I whipped my car around the corner going one row past the exit row and went down two levels on the opposite side of the lanes normally used for driving up, pulled into a spot, shut the car down, hiding amongst the other cars. Am I paranoid or what? Was that SUV aiming for me? Sure seemed like it. For the second time today, my heart was beating out of my head as I waited several minutes before pulling out and exiting the parking garage. Ever vigilant, I saw no sign of the black Escalade.

Sitting in my car in the gym parking lot, I brought Max up to date about Sam. I had no proof that the attack on Sam had anything to do with me besides speculation and Sam's declaration. He wondered why

Sam would be asking for me, and I had nothing to offer him except that we trained together twice a week. I told him that I would be returning to the hospital and checking on Sam until his sister arrived and trying to figure out why Sam thought his attack was related to me.

Max had some news for me too. He needed to travel to a previous installation site in Indiana because they needed help with some unexpected loose ends before he left town again to a Minnesota location to install the current project. He asked if I would be okay or if I wanted him to stay home. My situation seems precarious, but other than hiring a bodyguard, a constant companion, I had no idea what to do. Go into hiding? I don't think so. Max's schedule worked out for me because I wouldn't have to explain my actions, as no one would be around to question me.

I went in the front door of the gym and Charlene glared at me. Marissa just kind of turned her head and slunk out of the way as if to avoid certain doom. Charlene wasn't often mad or upset, just usually perky and accepting.

"What do you mean leaving me here all alone to open today? I was expecting you to be here before I got in," Charlene asked.

"Don't ask," I said and went in the office, grabbing a chocolate covered donut on the way, shutting the door to be alone for a minute. My story would disrupt the operations of the gym, and I needed to wait for a slow time because I couldn't start telling the story without finishing. I saw that Bob arrived and could assist at the front desk. Marissa slid into the office to check on me.

As it turned out, Charlene was late getting to work herself, so the real reason for her anger was that we opened late. Members were at the door waiting to get in, and she had to handle it alone.

Okay, not a great start to the day for anyone.

Later that afternoon, I explained what I knew about Sam's situation to our 'group of concerned' employees. Most of us had that open mouthed stare with little to say.

Marissa took me aside and strongly suggested I come up with a protection or offensive plan. The plan included a lot of what Rachel told me, but made sure that when I was home I would arm the alarm, and when I was out of the house I would always be with someone or someone would know where I was. Easier said than implemented, but I would try and I appreciated her concern, although I also worried that whoever was with me would be in danger.

I made my way back to the hospital and sat holding Sam's hand. Melinda came in and said that he was a little stronger and appeared to be out of danger. She told me she was going home, but was on 12 hour shifts and would be back tomorrow morning. I looked at Sam as Melinda left. Geez, if something about me caused this pain for him, how could I ever make up for that?

OverTheTop

Later that night, I sat with Matt silently too. We were comfortable together. No need to explain myself to him.

THIRTY

IN THE MORNING, I drove back to the hospital to check on Sam. When I got to the third floor, Melinda looked at me and said, "Unbelievable!"

"What?" I asked.

"That woman Amanda came charging in here last night demanding to get in to see Sam. She was higher than a kite on something. With the help of the Police Protection Unit, the staff was able to send her on her way. She tried to get in his room insisting she was his significant other. I don't think we've seen the last of her yet."

"No wonder Sam wanted to be protected from her!"

Sam was awake when I went into his room. We smiled at each other.

"Thanks for keeping Amanda out of here," he said.

"No problem."

"I am feeling a little better. Not great, but not comatose. Thanks for coming and checking on me. You know I care about you, and I know you are afraid of something inappropriate developing. I think 'we' could easily happen except for morals and ethics, right? What I want to say is that I think there is way too much coincidence going on in your life for these attacks not to be related. They seem to be centered on you, but there have been many distractions in the way, like the real estate scam and the Internet attack to throw us off track. Starting to look at all this from the viewpoint that it stems around you seems reasonable. I'm afraid for your life."

"What about yours? You were the one attacked this time. I'm fine with looking at this from all different angles. I don't have a better explanation even though I can't think of a reason I would be involved with your life, but thanks for caring and taking an interest."

"It's hard not to be interested when I've taken a bullet." He smiled slightly. "Just think. This could tie us together forever!" What a tease to the end!

I asked if he knew anything about some of the other members of the gym like Helen and Bill. He said he would check them out, but he thought they both moved to the area recently and maybe temporarily to check out the real estate deal.

"You should rest. Your sister will be coming this afternoon."

"So long as it's not my ex!"

"What's up with that?"

"She's crazy and would love to take my money and put it up her nose, sorry to say. She makes me scared for MY life."

"Gotcha."

I knew Sam was recovering nicely, and my mind could rest easier. Spending time taking care of business was next on my agenda.

I was designing the new membership drive. Marissa helped me with the brochures and fliers. Besides offering new members a choice of no enrollment fee, one month free, or a free six-week class, we were holding a drawing for people signing up. The winner of the drawing would receive a free membership. Yup, that's right. Whoever wins gets a free membership for a year. That's a lot of incentive to join! We put the options together in a nice, organized, appealing package that I was going to forward to Joe to put on our web page. I would also have some posters printed advertising the promotion.

When we finished the new membership drive task, I went back to Susan's training schedule to make sure all the 'loose ends' (her clients) were taken care of properly. The schedule was listed weekly with daily appointments by time within each week. There were a few gaps in time that I couldn't explain, but something was beginning to get my attention. I needed to double-check my idea when I got home.

I did a final check on Susan's locker to make sure it was cleared out and didn't have anything left with information that we could use. As I rounded the corner of the doorway, I saw Charlene moving something from her locker to her purse. Something that looked surprisingly like a gun. Charlene was packing!

"Charlene, what are you doing? You can't bring a gun to work here and keep it in the lockers. Also, when were you going to tell me that you got a gun? What kind is it? And do you need target practice? Where did you purchase it?"

Bob walked by the door and poked his head in to wave. Charlene and I didn't talk; we just waved back. I am past the point where I think all information needs to be made public, even to our inner sanctum. Charlene and I would talk guns later.

I went about my business checking out Susan's locker, and Charlene went to the front counter. Susan's locker was empty. Even though I expected nothing, opening the locker and finding nothing felt ominous. The lockers were metal, but had light oak finished doors on them. The inside of the locker rattled a little. I felt like she or someone was watching me. How weird is that? Watching me in the locker room?

Later at home, after I turned the alarm on, I pulled Susan's schedule and Mick's journal out, putting them side-by-side, finding the pages where the dates coincided with each other. I was right. The gaps in Susan's schedule coincided with the notes Mick made about being with Susan, but not showing any workout information. Maybe those guys were dropping it to the floor. Maybe Susan found out about the real estate scam or maybe Susan was helping Mick. Or maybe Susan and Mick were innocent and were trying to find out the truth. For one of those reasons, Susan had the two newspaper clippings hidden in her cookbook. The only thing that sounded right was that they were dropping it to the floor. I hoped they loved it, because that was some of the last fun either one of them had. Tomorrow I would check on her condo to make sure everything was okay.

Poor Matt. He wasn't getting a walk tonight. Instead, I made chocolate chip cookie dough and ate the dough, baking only a dozen of the cookies. I put the leftover dough in the refrigerator for tomorrow. Matt's a picky eater, but I gave him a little taste.

He ate it.

I went up to bed and surprisingly, instantly fell into a deep sleep.

THIRTY-ONE

I WAS IN that place between being awake and being asleep when I dreamed of wild, black dogs chasing me through a wooded area that never seemed to end. There was a cliff to my right and more woods to the left. I startled awake with my heart beating. Maybe the dream was trying to tell me I was afraid of something coming after me and I wouldn't be able to get away. Screw that! I was fighting back and going to find out who was responsible for all this mess.

After getting ready for the day at home and driving to work, making sure the gym successfully opened, I drove to the hospital to see Sam's progress. The day was cold and overcast making my emotions glum. The parking garage was filling up with people arriving for the day. I walked down the hall towards his room and saw a police officer seated in a chair outside his door. As I turned into the doorway of Sam's room, I noticed a woman standing over him. Her back was to me, but I could see she was tall and slim with thick, long blond hair. She wore jeans, black leather boots, and a cashmere sweater. A jacket hung over her arm. As she turned towards me, Sam introduced her as his sister, Victoria. She shook my hand, firmly, but coldly.

"If Sam's attack has anything to do with you, I don't know why you think coming here keeps him safe," she said.

"You may be right, but Detective Andrews has put a security detail on Sam until he finds out what happened. The attempt on his life may be totally separate from me. I want to make sure he is okay and am glad you are here to help take care of him."

Sam said, "Will you two stop talking like I wasn't here? It is what it is. We just don't know what yet." He shifted uncomfortably in his bed. "Claudia knows what I think about the incident. I just have to get strong enough to get out of here. The doctor said probably tomorrow. Victoria is staying in a hotel tonight. I hope the cops are done with my house so we can both stay there tomorrow night."

"I'm glad you feel ready to go home and Victoria is here to help you. I'll keep in touch to make sure you are recovering well. I'm headed back to the gym. Call me if you have any new ideas."

OverTheTop

When I got to the car, I dropped to the ground to check for bombs. Blowing this whole parking deck up would not be a good thing. I drove away from the hospital, through town to the MidTown Police Department. Chilly rain had settled in for the day. The police station was square, built with reddish brick, and had a circular driveway in front. I went up the concrete steps, pulled the door open, and asked the officer at the front desk if I could speak to Detective Andrews. The lobby area was pretty plain with beige walls, but displayed a large American flag. A side door opened and Detective Andrews motioned me to follow him. We walked down the tiled hallway into his office. Clutter covered the surface of the desk and his bookshelves.

"Have a seat," he said.

I got right to the point. "I think linking Sam to the rest of this is a mistake. There is no link to me other than personal training."

"Well, Susan was a personal trainer too."

"Yeah, but, the dots just don't connect for me. I want you to investigate alternatives to the theory that his attack has to do with me. The investigation should proceed as a stand alone crime."

He replied, "Some things don't connect, but with all the other incidences and two murders, I can't make pretend it isn't related to you. There would need to be two people to make Sam's story right. That's not to say there weren't two people involved with Susan and Mick. With Sam, someone had to be outside the window to make the noise and someone had to be inside to get him from behind, but his security wasn't on at the time."

"I think Susan and Mick might have been involved with each other." He raised his eyebrows. So I explained about the dates that were not related to the gym. I also told him about the real estate articles about Southern Life I found in her cookbook.

He leaned forward rather aggressively and asked me if I was withholding evidence. I told him that of course I wasn't and wanted everything solved as quickly as possible, but I was checking into some ideas and theories of my own, some thoughts that an outsider wouldn't connect.

"Maybe that's why someone wants you out of the way."

Grim, but true I thought.

"We will look at this from the perspective of Susan and Mick being together and whether they were involved in the real estate scam or were somehow part of it. Southern Life is one of the real estate companies that Mick did business with."

"I don't see Susan as doing anything illegal or being part of a scheme that complicated. I also don't see Sam as being part of the bigger plot. Whatever that plot is."

Driving back to work, listening to the rain hit the car, I decided to follow my instincts and treat this case as if Susan and Mick were together and innocent, leaving Sam as a separate incident.

OverTheTop

Mitch was waiting for me in the parking lot in her blue Audi 600. She got out of her car as I walked to the door. We went into the office, the only private place in the gym that had a door we could close to talk privately. She waited for me to talk first. I've seen that on TV too. Being silent often causes the other person to talk to fill in the quiet. I had a lot to say, ending up with my intention to pursue this debacle as Susan and Mick being together and Sam being not involved.

Mitch followed my logic and agreed to take a crack at the case using those parameters. She went on to say that she thought Helen might be legit and work in the mortgage finance business. However, she had doubts that even Harold Moore was a real alias for Bill Moody. The only reason anyone suspected him of any foul play was because of his seemingly over curiosity about Susan when talking with Bob. Without that, no one would be looking closely at him and discover he wasn't who he said he was. Was he in witness protection? Was he with the FBI? Was he a bad guy trying to salvage the real estate scam? Was he working to find out who was responsible for the scam? Was the scam much further reaching than MidTown? Mitch left, promising to be in touch.

I went back to business. The crew that maintains the equipment and machines for safety, regular maintenance, and required repairs was scheduled to be here in an hour. Marissa was close to completing the client and member databases; that was exciting.

She would show me how to access the information this afternoon. Charlene needed to leave for a doctor's appointment so I would be manning the front desk, as cheerful as always. I was hoping there was still a chocolate covered éclair in her donut box for me to scarf down when she left.

As members came and went, they commented on the rain. "I love it when it rains." "We needed the rain." "It's too cold for rain." "The worst weather is when it's forty and raining, like this." Someone once said we are all more alike than we are different. I often consider that, but today we seemed more different.

As Charlene left for her appointment, I told her she could take the rest of the day off. There were two éclairs left, and I ate both of them. The maintenance crew inspected and repaired the fitness equipment.

Marissa and I had time to go over her work. She showed me how to input, search, update, merge, print and make lists of information. This database would make membership and personal training much easier to follow and enhance making the information accessible and convenient. I was really proud of the work Marissa did and felt she helped the operations of the gym tremendously.

The afternoon grew quiet as the workers left and members finished their training sessions. Business would be slow until closing. There was a group yoga class scheduled early evening, the hour before closing. One 'yoga' member arrived in bare feet no matter what the weather or what time of year. Once I suggested that he had no idea what had been in that parking lot, so walking barefoot across it might not be a good idea. I think that offended him because he looked at me incredulously and told me the ground was fine and continued to arrive to classes in bare feet.

Getting ready to leave, I walked through the facility to make sure everyone was out, equipment was put away correctly, and power was shut off. Spooky and hollow is what the place felt like when it was empty. I quickly locked the front door, got in my car and drove home for the night.

Matt was happy to see me. His tail was wagging as he nuzzled my hand. After going to the bathroom in the backyard and eating his dinner, Matt curled up next to me as I vegged out reading my murder mystery.

Nancy Klotz

THIRTY-TWO

CHARLENE AND I arrived in the parking lot of OverTheTop at the same time the next morning. She hauled a bag of glazed chocolate donuts out of her car. The bag looked like it held enough donuts to feed an army. We unlocked the front door and started our opening up activities. Clients, members, instructors, trainers, they were all coming in at a steady pace. When there was a break in the activity, I asked Charlene about her gun.

"I am really getting uncomfortable with all the violence, threats, and ignorance with these cases. I mean, no one has answers. I feel I need to protect myself and took a class with this group of guys that teach self defense shooting, including how to use a pistol. They might have been mercenaries. They say if you're going to shoot someone even in your own home – shoot to kill. They teach that 1) you will be arrested regardless and taken in to the police department and 2) a criminal that's alive will come back to get you eventually. They told me if you shoot someone, tell the police that you are sick, like with a heart attack. They have to take you to the hospital and that will buy you some time to get help for yourself."

"Charlene, I get your frustration and I get your concern about life threatening events. I am with you on being able to defend ourselves. I just hope the paranoia is justified for us personally. Let's keep each other's back as much as we can."

"Oh and also, do you know anything about Susan and Mick's relationship?" I asked.

"As in relationship relationship? No, I thought Bob was hot for Susan and she spent some time with him," she said.

"I do think they did the deed in the stairwell from something he said recently. He was upset when we found out she was killed, but we all were. I think maybe Susan had moved on to Mick," I said.

Charlene replied, "You could be right. He was a regular, and they spent a lot of time training together. Besides, Mick was hot, he was successful, had a good life, AND he was single. Hmmm, real estate magnet versus personal trainer?"

I said, "If Mick was still alive, I'd think that Susan might have found out about the real estate scam and he offed her so she wouldn't tell, but they've both been murdered. I can't see them in the scam together, so maybe they were trying to find out what crimes happened and who was responsible. Or the murderer could think that Mick told Susan about the fraudulent leases. Client confidentiality only goes so far, right? Also, what about this Bill Moody person? Is he involved in the murders, the scam, or just way too curious?"

Charlene said, "I don't think we should talk about this in public or with an audience. Anyone could be involved or pass along something we've said to the wrong person. Knowingly or unknowingly."

"Good idea. I asked Mitch and Detective Andrews to look into Susan and Mick being together. Also, I don't see Sam as being part of this. How would killing him change anything?"

We got busy with people finishing their workouts and leaving along with the next shift of members coming in for their classes and sessions. Smiling, taking in cards and handing out keys, recording session information into our new database, greeting people using excellent customer service skills, and remembering to call people by their first names are activities of daily living when running a gym.

Later in the day, Detective Andrews came through the door and waited for me to finish with a customer who was purchasing a personal training package. I nodded to Charlene to take over, and we went into my one office. I sat in the swivel chair behind my small cherry wood desk and he took the Pottery Barn style chair with a nice burgundy and tan cushion for visitors. I call it the comfy chair.

"We found crushed grass outside the window of Sam's home office, like someone was stepping on it. Then there was a hollow spot on the cedar siding like maybe a baseball bat hit it. There's no sign of the bat. There's no sign of the gun, but a bat might have been used to hit him in the head first. That means there are two bats missing if the story goes the way he remembers. Sam's going home today. His sister is with him. We are going to station an officer out front for a few days and Sam promises to keep his security system on whether he's inside or gone."

"I'm glad he gets to go home, but hope it's safe. I'm wondering if his ex-wife and her crew have anything to do with the attack? Just saying. She sure showed up at the hospital quickly enough. Thankfully Sam had time to tell me to make sure she was not allowed in."

"We're checking all avenues. Who would benefit from his death? And why try now?"

All good questions I thought as he left to detect or whatever it was he did. I got a call from Mitch asking me to meet her at a local diner just outside the downtown area after I left work at 5 o'clock. I agreed, although, she didn't divulge the reason. That's Mitch – secretive, slippery, elusive, and informative.

Jacob's was a little restaurant not too far away from the gym. I drove out of town, up a small hill, and into the gravel parking lot. The single story building had seen better days and been around since before I was born. Jacob's was pretty well maintained, though, and had great burgers, fries, and sandwiches. As I entered, the wonderful smell of cooked burgers filled the air. Mitch stood up from a booth and signaled me to come over.

I said, "Aw shit," when I saw who was with her.

Bill Moody aka Harold Moore stood up, held his hand out and said, "Charles Stephens. FBI."

We shook hands, and I took a seat on the vinyl-covered cushion in the booth. A short and stocky waitress came over and placed the menus on the Formica tabletop. She was wearing the Jacob's uniform, a light blue dress with white puffy short sleeves and an apron in front. Kind of reminds you of the olden days like maybe when Jacob's got started. "Let me know when you are ready to order," she said.

"I'll start with a cookies and cream milkshake," I said.

Mitch ordered a diet coke. Charles wanted coffee, black.

"Well, alright, then," I said as I opened the menu.

"Pretty sure you're surprised, but when Mitch approached me, she assured me that you would keep this confidential, and you could be helpful," said Charles.

"The FBI thought did cross my mind, but I quickly discounted the idea. So what IS going on?"

"You did suspect me and give Mitch enough information about me for her to take a highly educated guess about what role I was playing in

MidTown even though she did not know exactly who I was. This real estate deal crosses many states and doesn't even originate here. Mick called a friend of his for advice when he discovered the skimming of the rent. He told Susan, and they discussed all the options and choices. Yes, they were together. Susan went out of her way to be discreet because she loved her job and knew how you felt about trainers and clients crossing the line. Mick's friend contacted an FBI friend, and eventually I was sent here to investigate, too late to keep Susan and Mick safe obviously. I was already working with Southern Life trying to find an 'in' to the scamming operation."

"Southern Life was the name of the company in the news articles hidden in Susan's cookbook," I said.

"Right. They seem to be the company creating and overseeing these fraudulent operations."

The waitress got tired of waiting for us to make a decision and came to take our orders. I like Jacob's because they have sweet potato fries. I ordered a regular cheeseburger, with a whole wheat bun of course, just to get the fries. Mitch and Charles ordered burgers with jalapeno pepper cheese and bacon with chipotle mayonnaise.

After the waitress left I asked, "Does Detective Andrews know about you?"

"Yes, but while we keep each other informed, we are working independently."

"Okay so why are you bringing me in on it?"

"First, I want you to stop hounding me. Put me as a 'low' priority in your research."

"Bob is the one that got your finger prints."

"Well you can de-emphasize me by saying you don't know how I could possibly fit in the current scenario. I'm just a nosey tourist or temporary consultant in town. Second, I want to know everything you know or think about the whole ordeal. You seem to have become a target here."

"Sorry, Mitch, but I am going to need to see this guy's ID. I've seen on TV how people impersonate the law to get information they want."

"You and your TV," Mitch said.

Charles pulled out his ID and I took my time trying to make sure it was real.

"Is there somebody I can call about you?"

"Aw, geez, Claudia. I already checked him out or I wouldn't have involved you. Or are you questioning me too?" asked Mitch.

"All right. All right."

The waitress came with our burgers. Mm, mm good. We ate silently for a while, then I disclosed all the 'evidence' I discovered like the fitness journal, the diary, the newspaper clippings, and what my speculations and theories were about Susan and Mick. I also told them that I didn't think Sam was part of the same series of crimes.

Then I asked, "What about Helen?"

"What about Helen?"

"Why were the two of you together?"

"We just went out for a drink. I wanted to get a feel for the local real estate market. Besides, she's intelligent, good looking, and works out! And she said yes when I asked her."

"So she's not part of this?"

"As best I know – no. This sounds to me like it might be more than one group of people. There's no consistent pattern or motive."

"No kidding."

With that, I left the diner to drive home for the evening. The days got dark fast and the darkness made me want to get in my pajamas early and never leave the house. This time of year is always hard to handle with daylight savings time making the days seem so short and the nights so long. We all start craving more food and heavier fare.

Matt was content to sit with me and follow me around from room to room when I needed to move. We watched a movie about a murder mystery involving a young woman and a psychotic ex-boyfriend. I went to bed as early as I could and still let the dog out late enough so I wouldn't have to get up too early in the morning because he was ready to use the bathroom again. My mind was grateful for sleep.

Nancy Klotz

THIRTY-THREE

SATURDAY IS ALWAYS busy at OverTheTop. The day was clear but cold. Fall leaves were still dropping and covering the ground with colors. By Thanksgiving, most of the leaves would be long gone except for some of the oak trees. I drove my handy dandy Rav4 to work listening to the weather on the radio.

I knew instantly that Charlene was already in the building when I pushed open the front door. The smell of fat, sugar, and chocolate permeated the air. Any kind of chocolate covered pastry that Charlene brought in was starting to seem appetizing to me. Forget the will power! She handed me one of the pastries of the day – chocolate covered cream puffs – and the calories just dissolved in my mouth. We agreed to eat lunch together in my office; the one private space in the building was becoming very popular. Bob was working the fitness floor and had some clients in the morning, including Beth McMan and Bill Moody. Bob would take over the desk during lunch. When you have a small business, employees often have to play many roles and multi-task in their jobs.

Charlene and I handled business as usual during the morning, greeting members, asking individuals personal questions about events going on in their lives, like injuries, births, family members, races they ran in, and adoptions becoming official. We exchanged membership cards for locker keys and handed out towels for the showers. I was glad we had a cleaning service coming in now to clean the showers, bathrooms, and towels. Group fitness people arrived, worked out, and left. Clients trained, accomplished personal bests, and felt successful.

When Bob came up front to take over for lunch, business had slowed down to a moderate pace. He asked us if we had heard any more information about Susan, Mick, or Bill Moody. He was disappointed when I replied not really. He seemed incensed that the police hadn't got any further with the case.

"I just can't BELIEVE that the police haven't found a suspect yet!"

I told him that Mitch hadn't found out anything incriminating about Bill Moody, so he probably wasn't a suspect either. That's our best bet.

I ordered in some turkey and avocado wraps, chips, and fountain drink diet cokes. Charlene and I went into my office, and she sat in the comfy chair while I took the swivel chair making me feel in a position of authority. We ate silently, not sure what to talk about.

"I talked to Mitch. I guess Susan and Mick were together. They discovered the real estate scam and were trying to figure out what to do. Perhaps that's why they were killed. She also doesn't think we need to worry about Bill Moody aka Harold Moore. Mitch says he's on the right side of the law. I still don't think Sam fits into the picture. What do you know?"

"One of our members, Jane Small, was mentioning how bizarre her morning was. She said her son and his friend found two baseball bats in the dumpster near my apartment. The Small's live in my complex. But then she went on to warn me to be careful because they saw blood on one of the bats and brought them to her. She called the police. She figures there's a mass murderer out there or at least a perp hitting people with a baseball bat."

"Detective Andrews was looking for two baseball bats in connection to Sam's attack. Thankfully they were found. The kids must have been a little freaked to see blood. I bet the blood is Sam's and hope the cops can get a some evidence from the bats," I said. "So let's continue to be on the lookout and piece some of this puzzle together."

OverTheTop

We finished lunch and returned to the front desk to relieve Bob.

"In what country is dueling legal?" he asked.

"Dunno," I said.

"Paraguay, as long as the duelers are registered blood donors."

"Huh," I said. That crazy Bob. He's cute and clever, that's what I say, but annoying at times.

Charlene stayed up front and I went back in my office to enter data into our new member database. So far Marissa and I have not trained the trainers how to update information so I input their receipts for training packages and any client information that was new. I planned a couple of different training sessions so everyone would have availability to attend.

My question to myself was about security of the system. Should I be concerned with trainers being able to view everyone's records, or should there be a code that limits them to only access their own clients? And what should I do when a client might use more than one trainer? I needed to decide fast and have the security measures in place or I would have to get Marissa back in to enter new data when I didn't have the time. I'm not sure why I am worried about security with my own employees, but with Susan, Mick, and Sam all being related to OverTheTop, I was a little concerned about who could get information from the system.

The office phone rang, and I picked up to answer. Sam was on the line and asked me what I was doing. I told him about my system security concerns. He said he contracted with a professional and capable security firm that would be able to check out the system and offer suggestions. I felt relieved that I didn't have to make those decisions by myself. He would send someone from the security firm to the gym.

I asked him how he was.

"Victoria and I are at my house; everything seems calm. Geez, I thought being in good shape would make me heal faster."

"Sam, it's only been four days. Give your body a chance to heal! You were knocked unconscious and shot. I still think you will get better quicker than the average person because you are so fit."

"Well, what can we research to find out more than we know now?"

"Sam, I don't think your attack was part of the scenario over here."

"What if it is?"

"Well, you may play a role, but what happened to you feels separate to me."

"Is that because you would feel really bad and guilty if I was hurt because of something that had to do with you?"

"Maybe, but the murders and crimes are so inconsistent. There is no pattern except that we are all related to OverTheTop, and there is nothing here important enough to cause all this chaos."

"Let's start with Susan," he said. "Do the police have her phone records? Who she called and who called her?"

"I'll ask Mitch if I can get a copy."

"What about Mick?"

"Ditto. What do you hope to find?"

"Not sure, just who they were in touch with."

"Did you know two boys found the bats in a dumpster by Charlene's apartment?"

"Andrews hasn't gotten back to me yet, but I expect to hear from him. Call me when you get the phone records."

We disconnected, and I called leaving a message with Mitch about wanting a copy of the phone records.

Driving home, I remembered it was Saturday night. Date night. Matt and I would be just fine hanging out together and going to bed early!!

Sitting in the backyard that night, I sensed I wasn't alone. There was a feeling of someone or something nearby, almost like a change in the wind or temperature of the air. I didn't see anyone, but went inside and made sure to set the alarm.

Thank goodness for Sundays.

THIRTY-FOUR

SUNDAY HELD NO big surprises, so I felt relatively calm opening the gym Monday morning. Monday was starting out as an ordinary day. Maybe as time passed, the answers would become clear. Murder and mayhem isn't something you can just ignore or believe will work itself out! Charlene and I finished off her chocolate covered donuts in fine fashion. In between members checking in and out, we secretly scarfed down the whole bag. My spandex stretched a little further.

Around 11 o'clock, I called Mitch on the phone, my purple nails tapping on the counter.

"Do you know Todd Horne's contact information?" I asked.

Mitch gave me the information and warned me not to do anything stupid.

OverTheTop

I told Charlene I was leaving for a while to scope out Todd Horne's territory. Charlene was beside herself. We agreed not to tell anyone about my shenanigans, but she wanted to make sure I wouldn't be alone with the guy.

The day was calm, but chilly. Clouds hung loosely in the blue sky. I got into my superb 6V four-wheel drive Rav4 and punched Todd's address into the GPS. I don't know what I was looking for, but knew what he looked like and wanted to figure out what kind of guy he was. I drove through town towards his neighborhood. He lived in an apartment complex that was next to a forest preserve. The buildings were three stories tall with one main entry door for all the apartments in each building.

Close by was a little strip mall with a convenient store, a veterinary, and a coffee shop. As I drove by the coffee shop, I thought I saw Todd inside. He was wearing jeans, a plaid shirt and a down vest. Being a personal trainer, he looked buff and like he must run or bike, a strength and cardio guy. I turned left around the corner and pulled into a parking spot. Now what was I going to do? He instantly recognized me as I entered the shop.

"Ah geez," he said. "What do you want?"

"I just want to talk."

"Well, I am out of an job, and I am still not giving anybody up."

"I just don't understand. Why would you want to put a personal attack on me? What have I done that deserves that kind of harassment?"

"Look, it's nothing about you. In the end it's about a few very immature twenty-something year old personal trainers that want more clients and thought OverTheTop would be a great place to get them."

"I don't know if you know about all the troubles going on in the MidTown world, but if you tell me what stuff these immature personal trainers are responsible for, I will not press charges against you for messing with me on the Internet."

"Yeah, I know about the troubles. I actually knew Susan and thought she was catching on to some of the plans these guys were making. They may have tried to warn her off. I only know that they might have painted graffiti on your building. And they might have approached some of your members trying to give them a better deal. In the end, they just don't get that being unprofessional doesn't get you clients, unless they are the sleazy ones."

If Susan knew about these 'immature personal trainers,' I wondered if they sent the letters to her at the gym and to her condo?

"You are the one trying to take me down on the Internet. Why are you referring to them as they?"

Todd was silent for a minute. Finally he said, "Well I got myself into a little money trouble. I like to spend more than I make and my credit card company got tired of waiting. I was just trying to make a little extra cash to keep the wolves away from the door, you know? I'm actually a pretty good trainer and PowerUp will lose some business with me leaving. But, my boss, Charles Johnson, was the one trying to undercut your prices in his advertising. That's just business."

"I get that money is hard to manage sometimes, but I don't get doing illegal and unethical activity to dig your way out. I won't push you, but thanks for the other information."

"You sure you don't need a new trainer at OverTheTop?"

Interesting dilemma for me. I'm all about giving people chances. I'm about kindness. Trusting someone who has gone against me is still a tough one though. It's like sleeping with the enemy. I smiled and told him we weren't hiring right now. I also shook a mental finger at myself because I illegally entered Mick's house. My justification was that no one got hurt and we were looking for helpful information. The police had already scoped the place out for evidence.

I was feeling a little warm and claustrophobic in the coffee shop talking with Todd. As I walked back to my car, the brisk air felt good and helped me clear my head. Back at the gym, Charlene and I strategized about what to do with the new information. We decided to make a checklist, like a 'to do' list, because now we had three items to cross off the master scheme of things – the letters, graffiti, and Internet. The remainder of the list was still pretty long.

Charlene sprang the rest of her strategy on me.

"Let's have a séance."

"A what?"

"A séance."

"And just who would we be calling back to speak with us?"

"Susan of course."

"And I suppose you know how to have a séance and how to communicate with the dead? I watch TV. There usually is just a one-word hint or a breeze blowing through the room. What could we possibly ask her to help us out with here?"

"Well at least you aren't totally against the idea," Charlene said. "I know a woman who is talented in that area."

"What area is that? What is the criteria for being talented? Is there a rating scale on the number of her successes with talking to the dead or what?"

"Don't be so cynical. I'm going to look into the possibility of having a séance."

"Shhh. Here come some of our members."

Later in the afternoon Marissa came in to work because Sam's security crew was evaluating our system. The head of the security team, Fred, was average. He was average height, average build, and average looking. He would easily lose himself in a crowd. The part of me that observed and described was at a loss. But Fred was outstanding when it came to security. He listened to our concerns and what we currently had. Marissa went through our computer system with him and showed him how it worked. He decided what secure upgrades would be effective and meet our needs. His crew was writing down what hardware and software we currently used. They were returning tomorrow to install the changes. Next he asked to go to my house.

"Hold on there. Sam didn't mention checking out the house. How much is this going to cost me?" I asked.

He smiled and said that Sam was covering the cost.

"That's not acceptable. I can't let Sam pay for these updates."

"Sam told me you would object, but he's already written the cost off to a security business expense account."

"Well, I'll need to talk to him about that."

"Okay, whatever you decide, but can we move on to your house so I can get started?"

Fred already knew where my house was so I actually followed him home. He had evaluated my neighborhood and the delightfully friendly cul de sac. Our back yard was fenced, but bordered five different back yards. Our lot was shaped like a slice of pie with the wide part in the back. From the outside Fred decided to install video monitoring that covered both sides and ends of the back yard as well as our patio. There would also be a monitor located in the 'black cat' tree that swept across the front of the house showing the windows and doors. These monitors were fairly invisible and connected to the main security system through Sam's KYX Company. Fred described the locks he wanted to put on the doors and windows and how the security system would be alerted if any of the openings were breached. His co-workers itemized a list of equipment they would need to get the job done.

Poor Matt. He had no idea what all the fuss was about and why these strange men were in the house. That reminded me that Max didn't either. Yikes.

After the KYX security team left, I took Matt for a short walk and came back to the house to settle in for the night. November was a good month for staying in because darkness came early making 7 PM seem like bedtime. Max called to check in before the real bedtime. I told him everything was fine and there were no worries. I suggested that Sam would like to check out our security system at work and home to make sure it was adequate.

"Why are you and Sam so involved with each other's lives all the sudden?" Max asked. "It's starting to feel like you have a new best friend."

"Well," I started slowly. "I'm not really sure, but I think with all the murder and mayhem that has been happening, we have both been victims of crimes. Attempted murder at least. We are part of a bigger picture until we get some answers about what has been happening. He's just concerned and taking precautionary measures. Besides more security is better for me."

"I'm concerned too. I don't always know how to help. I trust you to take good of care of yourself by training in self defense, improving shooting skills, and leaning on Detective Andrews and Mitch to work harder to get answers."

"I know sweetheart. I'm doing as much as I can. I love you. How's your day been?'

"Unfortunately, there are a few more difficulties at the plant than we expected and one of the plants in Idaho is having problems so I will need to finish here and go there before I come home. Are you sure you will be alright?"

"Of course, no worries. Sleep good."

"Thank Sam for his help. Sleep good too."

Poor Max. I hated that he had to travel so much because I knew he didn't like being gone. Now with all this stuff going on, he was feeling edgy.

I went to sleep right away. I slept through the night and woke up refreshed the next morning.

THIRTY-FIVE

THE KYX SECURITY crew arrived at the house early. I felt 'secure' in leaving them to do their installation as I drove to work. Tuesdays were mostly regular days. Nothing was ever spectacular about Tuesdays at the gym.

When I arrived, I called Mitch from my office to tell her to take the mystery of the letters, the Internet activity, and the graffiti off the list of things to investigate. I recapped my conversation with Todd and asked her to talk to our 'friend' Charles about removing those items from the concerns surrounding the real estate debauchery. Mitch seemed glad to get rid of a few worries but was on my case about not being careful and hunting down Todd. I reminded her that no one else was getting answers!

OverTheTop

As I hung up the phone, an important thought occurred to me.

"Charlene! Come in here!"

Charlene rounded the doorway with her bag of chocolate covered cream puffs.

"Pull up the Internet page that you were looking at about Sam," I said.

She came around the desk, next to me, and typed in a few search words.

"There," she said.

"See!" I said.

"See what???"

"Where was Sam's dog, Rover, during the attack and after?"

"That's a good question!"

I called Sam. Notice I have his direct line and he picks up right away.

"Where was Rover during the attack?"

"That's a good question! A neighbor called 911 when she thought she heard a shot. The police tell me Rover was outside when they got to my house. He didn't give them any trouble."

"What was he doing outside?"

"Someone must have let him out. Actually, someone must have forced him out quietly because I don't think he would just go out knowing I was still inside."

"Any ideas?"

"No, but I'll think about it," he said. "My next door neighbor kept him while I was in the hospital. How are you?"

"I'm fine, but we have to talk about all this security work you are subsidizing for me."

"No we don't. I just wrote it off to my security expense account. I feel better knowing I am doing something, anything at all, to keep you well. Knowing there are security measures in place means a lot to me."

"And are you keeping your alarm system on at all times?" I asked.

"Yes ma'am," he said. And we disconnected.

I looked at Charlene and asked her who she thought would make Sam a target and why. She hemmed and hawed a bit before saying she thought his ex-wife was involved. We couldn't figure out what an ex-wife would get from the death of an ex-husband other than revenge of some sort.

I never talked to Sam about Amanda, I had no idea if there were alimony payments, or if all the assets were divided, or if wills had been changed. Surely, the police would have asked questions like that. I'll have to get up my nerve to ask him what the Amanda situation looks like. According to Charlene, the divorce happened three years ago and there were no children. I guess at the time, his wife had been a successful actress in a daily soap opera playing the role of a manipulating hotty.

Over The Top

Forget getting my nerve up. What's that all about? I just called him right back. "What's your situation with your ex-wife?"

"Why are you interested?" he asked.

"I wonder if she had a reason to kill you."

"Oh geez, I thought you might be jealous."

"In your dreams."

"You are right. In my dreams."

My cheeks turned red. I could feel the blush. I'm glad Sam couldn't see my face.

He said, "We are completely divorced. The decree is fully completed. I can't think of a way she could get my money if I were dead. Although I imagine she would try."

"Wow. She must be a real treat."

"Actually she was an okay person before her addictions kicked in and kept kicking in. She rehabbed several times, but always the same result. Slowly I could tell she was getting a little sneaky or telling a few lies about her time and money and sure enough, she would be right back at it. Addictions are very scary and tough to beat."

"I'm sorry you had to go through that."

"I'm sorry for her because she had so much potential. I had to let her go; I couldn't keep supporting her habit. But she did know Rover. I'm surprised she hasn't kidnapped him and held him for ransom. I think I'll have the KYX security people run a check on her and see what's up."

After we hung up, I thought to myself, well, let's see, we have Detective Andrews from the MidTown Police Department, Mitch as a private detective, Charles Stephens as the FBI, KYX security, Sam, and me all working on the same case.

My phone rang again shortly after talking with Sam, and I noticed the callerid was Sam again. What now?

"Claudia, I have some news for you. Not good. Are you sitting down?"

"Sam, stop with all this drama and tell me what's going on."

"My KYX security team called me. Fred says he uncovered a recording bug and a video camera in your house as he was installing our equipment. Somebody has already been there putting in devices to watch and listen to you."

"OMG. Where were these devices located?"

"The audio bug was in the kitchen and there was a video cam in the family room. There was actually a bug in your home phone, too, although you may not use it much."

"How much more is going on around here that we don't know about?"

"Well the question is, do we want to get rid of the devices or try to use them to our benefit?"

"How would that help out? I don't even know who these people are or what they want. I can't even feed them misinformation because I don't know what information they want. I don't even know how long the bugs have been there. I think we should tell Detective Andrews at the very least and see if he has any suggestions. So Fred has left these 'bugs' intact?"

"Well he needed to cover up the fact that he was installing certain security measures in your home so the 'enemy' doesn't have all the goods. He ran some interference, but the devices are back in working order."

"This just pisses me off. My private life is nobodies business. I don't even tell family and friends stuff I don't want them to know. I'll call Detective Andrews, then you and I can take a little time to come up with a plan on how to use this invasion on my LIFE!"

After hanging up with Sam again, I spoke to Detective Andrews. He wanted time to think through the impact of removing the devices in my home and wanted more information before letting 'the bad guys' know we were on to them.

"This just gets interestinger and interestinger," he said. I didn't think that interestinger was a grammatically correct word, but it sounded good!

"What's up?"

"Well, I know you sent Mitch for phone records, but the police department isn't entirely incapable you know. On both Susan and Mick's phones, an app was used to delete the call records and history. They both placed calls to you before they died."

"Seriously? Really? That information just takes this case to a higher level of stupid." My temper was rising.

"Claudia, calm yourself down... now... Listen... Who ever is behind this thinks that Susan and Mick may have contacted you. That means they think Susan or Mick may have confided in you or told you what was going on. You have to think! What could you possibly know that Susan and Mick knew?"

"I don't know. If I knew, I would have shared, but I will get back to you if I think of something."

I immediately called Mitch and brought her up to date. She was hesitant to decide what her thoughts were on removing the devices. She wasn't sure we were ready to show our hand yet.

"Listen, if these people thought I was the 'go to' person, then they don't know another friend was contacted who ended up getting Charles involved. So the crimes must have to do with the real estate scam."

"That would have the biggest impact on money. You know what they say – crimes are committed for money, sex, power, or religion. I'll talk to Charles."

After we hung up, I had this nagging feeling that I was missing the very thing that was right under my nose.

What a day. At some point, I would actually have to get some real work done. I was going home to Matt. We were staying out of the family room and resting quietly tonight, that's for sure.

THIRTY-SIX

THE NEXT BRIGHT and perky morning, Charlene reminded me that our bi-annual locker cleanout was the next weekend. It was Wednesday, and from here until Saturday, we would be asking members to leave the lockers unlocked as they left the gym for the day.

Members leave the lockers empty, but may lock the door. Most lockers were used on a day-to-day basis, although we did have a group of people who wanted permanent lockers as a place to keep their stuff year round.

Twice a year we had a crew look through and clean the inside of the lockers from trash, dirt, and whatever else ended up being left behind. The more lockers that were left unlocked by the members meant the fewer lockers we would have to come get keys for to open up during cleaning time.

Bob was as bright and perky as the morning. He walked up to the front counter and asked, "What are the dots on the side of a domino called?'

"Dunno," I said.

"Pips."

"Huh."

Will that Bob ever end? Most people find him quite charming. I'm just not in the mood, but I am working on my attitude because customer service is the number one thing that will make or break member loyalty. I need my smiley face on today and everyday.

Later that afternoon, I could hardly remember what I did up until that point. I was totally absorbed and preoccupied. Talk about not being in the present moment! My mind kept processing and reprocessing all the information about each incident that happened in the last several weeks. And here I was lecturing Bob and Charlene about staying focused!

My phone rang. Sam again.

"I think you were right," he said. "KYZ Security research showed that Amanda still has a $100,000 life insurance policy out on me that was paid five years in advance. Of course, she is the beneficiary.

Detective Andrews called me a few minutes ago to say that the blood and hair samples on one of the two baseball bats those kids found are mine. He also said they found a good partial fingerprint on one of the bats that matches the prints of a schmuck dealer called Shorty. I bet that nickname pisses him off!

Shorty is also a user. Big mistake. Anyways, they bring this guy in and he is happy to tell the story because he was the one outside of the house banging the side with a baseball bat to create a distraction. He figures if he cooperates with the investigation, he will get in less trouble than if the cops find the other players and they try to pin it on him. So do you have a minute to meet?"

"Alright."

"Okay, let's meet over at the police station because Andrews will show us the video of Shorty's interview. Can you be there in 15 minutes?"

"Sure."

I asked Charlene if she could stay and close up if I didn't get back in time and drove to the police station. Sam was waiting in the parking lot and we walked into the front lobby together. The desk sergeant called for Detective Andrews. Sam and I really didn't have much to say to each other, and Andrews didn't take long to come and get us. He escorted us down the bleak hallway to an interview room on the right. The walls were painted beige on concrete, and there was a basic conference table with four uncomfortable looking metal chairs with padded seats. A computer was sitting on the table. The three of us pulled our chairs around to face the screen, and Detective Andrews pressed the play button.

Shorty was short. I have always heard that some men can't take being short and think they have to act big to compensate for their size. This guy was shifty and nervous, tapping his toe and bouncing his knee. His thin black hair was wispy around his face and sweaty forehead. He had on gray cargo pants and a blue plaid button down shirt with the sleeves rolled up. His eyes moved back and forth as he talked. He told the story of how he hung around Amanda and a few other people. They were usually strung out and a couple of weeks ago were trying to figure out how to get their next fix. Amanda said if Sam were dead, she could collect the life insurance money. Someone else asked what was up with the other two people who were killed recently at OverTheTop. Amanda brought it back around to herself saying that they both went to the gym where Sam worked out. Buster came up with the idea of taking out Sam to make his murder look like it was related to the other two deaths. The conversation was a brainstorming activity by people with little brains left, which somehow ended up being a real plan.

Shorty didn't want to be a part of a real murder, but the whole idea seemed 'surreal' in his mind. Buster staked out Sam's house until he found a time when Sam was going to be home. At that point, Amanda distracted the dog, Rover; Shorty distracted Sam's attention out the window; Buster came up behind him and finished him off. They quickly cut through the back yard onto the next block, dispersed, and met up an hour later at their regular hang out place on White Street. Shorty took the bats and threw them out in a neighboring dumpster.

OverTheTop

Detective Andrews stopped the video. "Shorty is still in the can waiting for us to figure out how to prove all this and find Buster and Amanda to bring them in."

"Well, Shorty is very enlightening, that's for sure," said Sam. "I'm so disappointed in Amanda. There's not much left for her if she is involved like this."

"I'm sorry, Sam." I didn't really know what to say to him about his ex plotting to have him killed. That kind of topic just doesn't come up every day.

"We will keep you updated as we track down this story," said Detective Andrews.

Sam and I walked back out through the building into the parking lot.

"Well, you're alive and now you don't have to worry about being apart of whatever this other case is all about!" I said.

Sam scowled.

"You just don't get it. You are involved in something very serious, and the danger is not over for you. You need to be aware!"

He slammed his car door and drove off. Yeah, like he wasn't just involved in something very serious and dangerous...

I checked my watch for the time, 5:30, and decided to go home and let Charlene close up. I've had enough of this day.

Matt and I played in the backyard as he did his little run around dance. Then he faithfully stopped and sat by my side so I could rub his ears. Unconditional love is a good thing. As I watched Matt I remembered how he always looks at the world through new eyes with interest and awe. Maybe that's a technique I could use to think about this mess I'm in.

Max called that evening asking how I was. I told him everything was fine and that Detective Andrews promised to keep in touch as they investigated the case. I knew Max was tired. He works very hard and long hours when he is out of town. Usually I just don't bring up bad news when he's gone. A lot of times the bad news is over with by the time he gets home, and he never needs to know about it. We don't always have a full disclosure relationship.

THIRTY-SEVEN

THURSDAYS AT THE gym can sometimes be like Tuesdays, just regular. For some reason, people try to make a Monday, Wednesday, Friday schedule and usually come Monday because either they want a good start to the week or they blew their goals over the weekend. Many of them make Wednesday, but not so much on Friday, unless of course Tiger Lady is teaching. Although, there are some who are trying to be realistic and come two times a week so they pick the Tuesday, Thursday schedule.

Charlene arrived with her deep fried chocolate donuts. We weren't discussing the nuts and bolts of the case too much anymore, but enough so that we both had all the pertinent details. We have each other's back. Charlene told me she talked with her séance talented friend, and they were planning to have coffee together to discuss the situation, Susan, and expectations. The séance friend wanted to know what outcome we thought we would get from communicating with the dead. I'm guessing she would be asking what our preconceived notions of a séance were.

Cindy and Terry were here training clients today. They had a steady flow of people coming and going. Making a living in the fitness industry is hard, especially until you made a good solid name for yourself. First, you don't get paid if a client doesn't show up. Training is expendable when people don't want to part with their money. Then, keeping people motivated and consistent is an issue. A client could be making a lot of progress and have something happen in life that totally throws them off. Or falling off schedule could be as simple as a client missing two sessions and then not getting back in to the routine.

I decided to offer a Thanksgiving special of buy 5 hours get one free. That's a big deal. I was going to wait until December to offer gift-giving specials. If members were waiting to buy packages as gifts, filling in revenue sources for November might be difficult. I was working out the fine details and not so fine details of the special offerings when Mitch appeared.

"I'm full of news, so we better go in your office," she said.

"No," I said thinking of the bugs at my home. "Let's walk down to the coffee shop. I'll find someone to cover the counter."

November can be in the 20's or the 70's in the Midwest. Today was an overcast coat and hat day, but not so cold as to keep you inside. We quietly walked to the coffee shop and ordered. There were several people in the shop working on their computers enjoying the Wi-Fi and Internet connection. I got a peppermint hot chocolate with skim, no whip. Mitch got an espresso with cream. We actually went outside and found a bench near the Riverwalk. The air was still for a change, no brutal winds blowing through.

"I've been working with Charles a little bit. The real estate bad guys think Susan and Mick came to you with their information, not Mick's friend. They know someone was contacted. These guys don't know about Charles being here to work the case. Who knows why they think you would be the one Susan and Mick would contact. Someone erased those phone calls to you and that indicates they were considered important. Those erased calls are like a beacon and if so, it was a really big mistake to erase them.

I was doing a little surveillance for Charles and I was in a position to overhear what two of the real estate goons were talking about. I don't think they took Susan and Mick out. I think they don't know who did it either and they are worried about who did and what impact the killer(s) could have on their scamming operation. They think it may be a territory move or a threat to warn them off by another group of conspirators. By the way, I say goons, not to write them off, because they are very dangerous, but to say they aren't at the top of the ladder intellectually. They are getting some heat from whoever hired them, but they have no idea what is going on."

"That makes all of us then," I said.

"Since 'the goons' don't know what you know, they figured it was easier to just take you out. But the bomb didn't work and put everyone on alert. So they set up surveillance in your home."

"I need KYX Security to check for bugs or videos in my office at work or behind the counter actually," I said.

"Originally, they just tried rattling your cage with the black cat. I think black shoes was trying to find who offed Susan when he came to her condo. Then the guy at the cemetery was trying to warn you off or threaten you. They wanted to remind you they were still watching and close by."

"This leaves a lot of open ended questions. If you are right, I do need to start looking at all the evidence with new eyes, just like Matt."

"Matt?"

"Yes, my dog. I'm going to follow his example."

"Well, alright then. Let me know how that works out for you."

OverTheTop

"What do Susan and Mick and I all have in common? Besides OverTheTop?"

"Good question. Now use those new eyes of yours to think about the answer."

We walked back to the gym in silence. A little breeze was picking up after all. With the cool temperatures and overcast sky, getting inside became a priority. I was chilled to the bone.

I knew that on the way home I was going to get a bag of candy corn. I love candy corn; it's pure sugar. I love chocolate more, but this time of year, candy corn was easy to get. Those corns just chew up and go down so easy, handfuls at a time! I would probably eat the whole bag in one day. That's what I do. If sweets are around, I eat them. Sometimes, I have to shake them out of the bag into the garbage can, the can in the garage, to stop myself. If I don't think I will stop from picking them out of the garbage, I put them down the garbage disposal in the sink. Tonight I was going to give into fate and know that I would eat the whole bag.

Matt likes candy corn. Last year Max would toss a candy corn in the air and Matt would catch the candy in his mouth and eat it. We videotaped him. I'm not sure how many candy corns poor Matt will get this year because my hand is in the bag!

Nancy Klotz

THIRTY-EIGHT

FRIDAY WAS JUST gray and cold. The wind was blowing and the cold seemed to invade my privacy. I drove to work with my seat warmer on. The warmer hardly had time to heat up properly. Friday morning classes went as scheduled. We sold several of the 5-hour training specials. They didn't expire, so technically these packages could be bought as gifts for the holidays as well. If a member already had a trainer, the pair would determine the schedule together. If someone was starting out as a new client, we would find a trainer that had a similar schedule to the client's timeframe needs. Then that trainer and client would have a consultation to determine goals and fitness needs. Forms like Assumption of Risk, Informed Consent, and Waiver of Liability would be filled out. The client fills out the Health History Form.

OverTheTop

Sometimes the truth doesn't come out about health history until later in the training when the client becomes more trusting of the trainer. There's not always total disclosure in this relationship either.

Rapport was also very important. The client needs to feel comfortable enough with the trainer to give the sessions a go. Fitness testing is scheduled if a client wants a baseline to compare against for accountability and measurability or if a trainer determines the information is necessary for program design. Often a participant isn't interested in a fitness assessment.

Friday is Sam's regular training day. I kind of miss him being here. Sometimes you don't know how important something is until you don't have it anymore.

"Charlene, tell the trainers to clean their lockers out if they keep belongings in them overnight. If they want the cleaning crew to wash their lockers, each person can label one of the leftover cleaning supply boxes with their name and store their locker stuff in it over the weekend."

"Okay," Charlene said. "I'll actually type up a little reminder to put in each of their mail folders."

"Charlene, you are just so efficient! What would this place be like without you?"

"Yikes! Don't ask that question! We are already down three people!"

"Sorry."

Bob stopped by the front counter and asked, "Sorry about what?"

"I just made a bad joke. It doesn't matter," I replied.

The day passed slowly, but without any big event, so I was okay with slow. I drove home to see Matt and make some peppermint tea. I felt like hunkering down and sitting quietly. The days were dark by 4:30 now and bedtime seemed to start before the gym even closed for the night.

Saturday morning was time to go right back to work. Rain was the name of the game. Although, the weather was warmer than normal, so 50 and raining is better than 40 and raining. I'm sure we would be getting snow before too long.

I put on my standard issue spandex with a fitted wicking long sleeved blue shirt and my gym shoes, covering up with an OverTheTop logo sweatshirt and my raincoat. Matt went out in the rain to do his business before I left. Then I was gone for the day. Sometimes Marissa or Steve came by during the day to let Matt out or keep him company.

Saturday was busy as usual. There's not much downtime, but every once in a while I would find myself thinking about how to get the killer(s) to come out when we had no clue who they were or what their motivation was. Later in the day the locker cleaning crew came in to go through the lockers that were open and not being used for the day. I was closing up that night. The supervisor of the crew was going to call me when they finished so I could lock up after they left.

I came back in around 9 o'clock that night. The building is a little spooky when you are alone at night. I checked the locker room out. All the locker doors were open and the insides clean. As I started to leave, I remembered the trainers' lockers and went to make sure they were clean. One of the lockers was still locked, and I went to find the key at the front counter. Because the key I was looking for was missing, I took the master key for that set of lockers and opened the door. What a mess. Oh, geez. I realized this must be Bob's locker because I recognized some of his stuff. I never realized he was so messy. I was really hoping there was no food left in there. I kind of checked around without displacing or touching too many items. At the bottom, I saw the edge of a zip lock bag. I lifted the sweatshirt on top to see if there was food, and something shiny caught my eye. As I pulled the snack sized bag out, I noticed a gold chain inside. The word 'Susan' was written on the gold heart on the chain. Uh oh. There must be a reasonable explanation for this, but how would I find out without him thinking I was going through his stuff? I watch TV. I wiped the bag clean of my fingerprints and slid it back under the sweatshirt with just the corner sticking out like I remembered. I locked the door, replaced the master key, and drove back home feeling perplexed.

Sunday was a day off, but I called Mitch after making a cup of coffee. Sitting down at the kitchen table, I told her about the gold chain I found in Bob's locker.

"And of course it was reasonable for you to look through his things to make sure there wasn't any food left in the locker," she said.

I really thought looking for food was reasonable and didn't even know the locker was his until I opened the door.

"Did the necklace look like it was worn, used, or shiny new?" she asked.

"Geez, I didn't even think to notice."

"Well, what are the scenarios? 1) Bob could have bought the necklace for Susan and never gave it to her. 2) He could have found it and not known what to do with it. In which case, he could have given it to Susan's mother. 3) Susan's grandmother could have given it to Susan at her 16th birthday party, and she wore it ever since. Bob wanted something of hers as a memento. 4) He killed her, and it is a trophy."

"Hmmmm. Those are tough choices....Look, if Bob killed Susan, who killed Mick? I thought we determined that these murders are related. And why would Bob kill Susan?"

"I don't know."

"Well, I am going to dig around a little to try to find out more information."

"Don't do anything stupid."

Famous last words.

OverTheTop

Matt and I went for a brisk walk. He loves running back and forth across the sidewalk when we are in the neighborhood. Consequently, he covers a lot more distance than I do on our walks.

Max called and said he should for sure be home Tuesday night. The installation project was coming to a close and problems in another plant were getting resolved. He always seems to be needed somewhere. I have asked him about trying to delegate his responsibilities or to train someone to replace himself so he could have a little free time and not travel as much. He doesn't really listen to me. He always has a reason why he does what he does. I feel like I'm trying to be helpful; he feels like I'm trying to be critical. I stop talking so much and just listen. Well, we can have a good snuggle when he gets home.

I made some chili with noodles and cheese for dinner. Reading a good book is always a nice distraction from life. Your brain grinds away in the background, but if you are intrigued with the story, you don't notice your mind chatter as much. After reading for an hour or so, I fell asleep with the book still by my side.

Nancy Klotz

THIRTY-NINE

MONDAY MORNING STARTED as a nice fall day, blue skies, sunshine and 45 degrees. I dressed warmly in my black spandex pants and wicking shirt. Many of the fall leaves were down reminding me that winter was close at hand.

When I arrived at the gym, I took care of business as usual, but kept an eye out for a time when I could casually approach Bob. Charlene was eating chocolate cream puffs when she thought no one was looking. Members were coming and leaving. The phone was ringing. I could hear the clank of weight machines and dumb bells. Two hours later, I saw that Bob was alone and taking a break sitting on one of the benches. With total innocence I sat down beside him.

"Has everyone quieted down about Susan?" I asked.

"What do you mean?"

"Well, you mentioned Bill Moody being more curious than most. I wondered if her death still concerned many people or have they just taken it in stride and moved on."

"No, most people don't mention her too much anymore."

"Well, I guess that's good for business, but sad for Susan."

"Yeah, sad for Susan."

I pressed my hands on my thighs to stand up and walked back towards the front counter.

Later that day, in my most innocent way, I asked Charlene what she knew about Bob and Susan's relationship. Surprisingly, she didn't know too much. Charlene chatted up to most everybody. She knew they worked well together and that they may have hung out together for a short while, but that's about all. She chuckled saying they probably christened the back stair well, but called the encounter casual sex.

Monday was my night to close, although I wanted to stay anyway. Charlene was waiting for me so we could walk out together. I told her I needed to get something in the locker room. With key in hand, I opened Bob's locker. What a surprise! The locker was cleaned out with only a folded sweatshirt and extra pair of socks stacked neatly on the bottom. A small mirror was attached to the inside of the door along with a small basket containing a comb and a key resting inside. No necklace. As I shut the locker door again, Charlene was leaning in the room and said,

"Remind me not to leave anything I don't want you to see in my locker."

I didn't know if she knew about the necklace or if she just thought I was being nosy, so I ignored what she said, and we started heading out the front door.

On Tuesday, I knew Max was coming home. Time for researching Bob was either now or tomorrow during lunch. I slowly drove by Bob's apartment. No lights were on and I didn't see his Jeep in the parking lot. I drove by slowly from the other direction, turned around and parked a block away so I could see any activity. After about twenty minutes, Bob drive up in his burgundy Jeep Wrangler. He parked, got out of the car, walked up the sidewalk and stairs, and went into his apartment. I saw a light go on.

Dang! Now what was I supposed to do? I could treat him like a suspect and come back tomorrow during lunch, pick the lock on his door and go through his belongings. What was I looking for? Or I could walk right up those steps and knock on the door and ask him about the necklace. I mean Bob is Bob. I wasn't planning very well because I had no idea what his schedule was like for tonight anyway. Was he in for the night or going back out? Sneaking in tonight wasn't likely when I didn't know how long he would be away if he left. I started up my car and drove home to Matt.

Potato skins for dinner was my current favorite 'go to' meal when Max was out of town. I like not having to cook for someone all the time, although Max does help out cooking meals. Matt ate his dinner and came to sit by me. I rubbed his ears. He never used to like having his ears rubbed when he was younger. He's getting mellow in his older age. Tomorrow I would check out Bob's apartment during lunch when I knew he would be at the gym.

I went to sleep for the night confident in my decision.

The next morning I dressed in my standard issue spandex and purple long sleeve wicking shirt. For variety, I changed the earrings I usually wore. When I entered the front door of OverTheTop, I instantly knew something was up. I could hear the buzz in the air. The local daily news on the Internet covered the story of Sam Good. His ex-wife, Amanda, and another of her strung out friends, Buster, were arrested for attempted murder. Charlene played the video for me that showed Amanda and Buster being lead from the squad car to the police station in handcuffs. I wondered how Sam felt. I was secretly delighted that his attack had nothing to do with my situation. Although, his attack brought him into my life, and with his security team, I was protected and found out valuable information about the case.

I still didn't know what to do about the surveillance at my house. Matt and I were careful to stay out of sight and were quiet around the audio bugs. Max was coming home tonight. Yikes! I better decide to either tell him or get rid of the cam and bugs.

Tuesdays at the gym are Tuesdays at the gym. I waited until Bob had returned from lunch to go to lunch. His neighborhood was about three miles from the gym, like mine, but in another direction. His apartment complex was neat and clean, but not new. The rust stained cedar and brick buildings were two stories tall with apartments on the bottom and on the floor above.

The parking lot was nearly empty, but there were a few cars remaining. I wondered if these were babysitters, unemployed workers, or the night shift. I really didn't want to be seen or call attention to myself so I parked where I did the night before and pulled on ball cap on to cover my blond hair.

I strolled up to his apartment building like I belonged there. After climbing the stairs and finding his door, I pulled out my credit card and wiggled the edge vertically in the crack between the frame and the door. I tilted the card towards the doorknob until it slid in a little farther. As I bent the card the opposite way, I could feel the lock slide, my card holding the lock back only long enough for me to open the door. I slowly pushed the door praying that he did not have a security system.

I didn't hear an alarm, not that there wasn't one. As I surveyed the walls, I didn't see an alarm box. I stepped lightly, only on my toes as I moved from room to room, not really knowing what I was looking for. His apartment was sloppy, almost like a college apartment, except he didn't let old food pile up and make the air smelly. The dishes were piled up, just not the food. The walls were apartment beige, with just a few pictures hanging. The furniture was worn woven upholstery with blues and browns. A couch and a matching recliner faced a flat screen TV resting on a glass TV stand. Overall, nothing looked old and ruined, but nothing looked expensive and new either.

I made my way to his bedroom, thinking the necklace might be in there. Why did I need to find it? I don't know, but if I did, I was going to take a picture with my phone. His queen-sized bed was unmade and the pillows were strewn on the floor. His wooden dresser was pretty clear on the top except for a box that would have reminded me of a jewelry box if Bob were a girl. I put on gloves and opened the box. The necklace wasn't there, just a few trinkets that didn't seem worth much.

I tiptoed towards the walk-in closet and opened the door. Wow! Jackpot! Scary jackpot! There was a small oriental style wooden chest against one of the walls. On it were several pictures of Susan along with the heart necklace and a ring with what looked like a garnet stone in the setting. The chest looked like a shrine of sorts. I quickly took a picture with my phone and then hightailed myself out of there making sure no one obvious was outside to see me and checking to be sure that the door locked when I closed it behind me.

Reminding myself to act like I belonged there, I walked back to my car, got in, locked the doors, and took a long deep breath in and out. Not wanting to be seen in the neighborhood, I drove back to my house to calm down a little before returning to the gym. Matt was happy to see me. I gave him a milkbone. He is a picky eater, but he ate the bone and somehow that grounded me.

Before returning to the gym, I slowly and quietly removed the 'enemy' surveillance devices, piled them up on the patio and smashed them by repeatedly stomping them into the paver stones. Now the 'enemy' would know that the bugs were discovered.

I threw some meat and vegetables into the crockpot so dinner would be ready when I got home and left for work. Now, do I have a poker face or not? I do not know, but according to me, my expression was totally natural any time I had contact with Bob for the rest of the afternoon.

Max was home when I returned. The house smelled delicious from the stew in the crockpot. We hugged and held on to each other for a good long while. He had been gone several days and we always feel good together when he gets home. He feels solid and stable, safe. I assured him that the case was still in progress, but no new news. We both knew what was coming later that night. An orgasm or two are always helpful for a good night sleep.

FORTY

MAX AND I slept in until 8 o'clock. Getting out of a warm, snuggly bed was hard. We ate breakfast and had a cup of coffee together and caught up on the news of his work and some of the happenings around here while he was gone. He went out to catch up on some errands and I left for work. I was closing tonight.

Charlene was dressed in orange and black as the season was still fall. She brought in chocolate covered donuts with orange and black sprinkles on top. Eating habits always seem to change when stress levels go up. We both ate two donuts. Bob had the day off, so I figured Charlene and I would eat the last two sometime before the day was over.

On Wednesdays, members came in with good intentions for reaching their weekly workout goals.

We had a steady flow of members and clients, and we ordered in sandwiches, chips, and diet cokes for lunch. The day was nice with just the two of us working to collaborate and provide excellent customer service. That and two orgasms the night before made for a calmer, mellow day.

Mitch dropped in and we found an open, empty space to talk. She told me that Charles Stephens had enough evidence gathered to bring the two bombers of my car into custody. He was having them watched to make sure they weren't planning something dangerous right away. He wanted to figure out a way to get to the bigger guy – their boss or their bosses' boss – to put an end to the real estate scam. I'm not sure how comforting that news was to me.

I showed her the picture of Bob's shrine, and then sent it to her phone. We still weren't sure what to think of his apparent obsession with Susan. If Mick's and Susan's deaths were related, what was the deal? I also told her I got rid of the listening devices and the video cam before Max came home. That made her a little nervous, because no one knew how the 'bad' guys would react when they knew they were found out.

After the 6:30 cardio class was over, members trickled out and I let Charlene leave a few minutes early. Taking a visual sweep of the building to make sure everything was in place, I started towards the front door when it opened. Bob walked in.

"Hey, Bob. What's up? I'm surprised to see you here."

"I bet you are."

"What do you mean?"

"One of my neighbors took a picture of you with her phone standing at the door of my apartment. The time stamp was after my lunchtime. And seriously? The night before you were parked on my street."

"Okay."

"You were there nosing around yesterday. How could you come into my apartment like that?"

"Well, my curiosity got the better of me, but you have no proof that I went into your apartment. I was checking out where you lived."

"Why is that?"

"When we were locker cleaning, your locker was never opened, so I unlocked it and saw a necklace of Susan's in there and wanted to know why."

"Why didn't you just ask me?"

"I don't know. I didn't know if you were a suspect or a broken hearted lover. Enough threatening events have taken place that I just am not taking anything for granted anymore."

"Well, you just should have believed in me. Then this all could have ended with Mick and been over with. I can't let you keep nosing in my business or telling anyone about what you saw so they start asking questions too."

"So what is going on, really?" I asked. "What is Susan's gold necklace all about?"

"I loved Susan. Still do. She was so fresh and positive. Being around her was like being on top of the world."

"It's okay to love someone. I'm sorry for your loss. Why do I think there is a but… here?"

"But as soon as that Mick showed interest, she dropped me like a hot potato and never looked my way again."

"That must have hurt. Must have felt like a betrayal."

"It did. A lot. I confronted her out on the Riverwalk and she just blew me off. She made it sound like what we had was just a brief interlude, a casual moment in time. I felt like she was laughing at me as we sat at the edge of the river."

"What happened, Bob?" I was getting this eerie, worried feeling that I might not get out of this alive. I was desperately trying to think of an escape route while trying to keep him talking. Was this guy the real Bob? I never saw it coming.

"I shut her up. I bashed her head with a nearby rock. I pushed her over to the edge of the river out of sight and threw the rock in the water. I came right back to OverTheTop, business as usual."

"I can understand you feeling angry and hurt by her. But how does Mick fit in and what happened there?"

"I think Mick knew I killed her because I warned him off of Susan. He didn't have any proof. They both knew I expected them to stop seeing each other.

Besides, he had been with her, and that was enough of a reason for me to shut him up."

"You really went out of your way to make the murder look suicidal."

"Yeah, well, I didn't want the two killings to appear connected, now did I?"

"So now what?"

"They both tried to call you to warn you about me and my threats, but I knew they hadn't gotten to you yet. When this real estate scam came up, it was a perfect way to set them up as victims of a crime."

"You are quite a creative, masterful guy, Bob."

"Well, now you know." He pulled a gun and pointed it straight at my forehead. Yikes! Where was my gun? Still in my purse.

"So you're going to shoot me now? Come on, Bob."

"Oh yeah, everyone will think it was whoever tried to blow you up. This is so easy!" He clicked the safety off.

"Hold it," shouted Mitch. Where the hell did she come from?

Bob turned towards her and took a shot. She shot him in the hand that held the gun. As he swung around and tried to grab me with his free arm, she shot him in the opposite shoulder. He went down cursing and screaming Susan's name. I grabbed the phone and dialed 911.

Geez, blood was everywhere. I never really knew how distinctive the smell of blood was.

Detective Andrews quickly arrived along with an ambulance. He must work 24/7. He went along with Bob in the ambulance to the hospital to question him and ensure he got medical attention. The police department put an officer to guard him, I think mostly from escaping.

Detective Andrew's side kick, Detective Mulligan, stayed behind to get the story from Mitch and me. Mulligan was fair skinned with freckles and red hair. He was wearing a trench coat and had a visible shoulder holster. He was probably 35 or so, a mere babe compared to Andrews and me. Mulligan directed the crime scene crew when they arrived. The gym was going to have to close down for a few days. What a mess! I called Max, and he came to be with me until I was free to go.

"You sure provide excitement and adventure in life," he commented. Then he gave me a squeeze on the shoulder and pulled me into a hug.

Mitch told Detective Mulligan that during a scheduled locker cleanout, I had come across a gold chain with a heart that was engraved with Susan's name. She felt that the necklace was enough cause to check Bob out and start some surveillance on him. During such time as she was watching him, he came to the gym after hours and entered the building. Knowing that my Rav4 was still in the parking lot, she slipped inside the front door quietly to see what was happening. Hidden behind the counter, she listened to our conversation and stayed out of sight until Bob pulled his gun. At that time she feared for my life.

I told Mulligan that I found the necklace in a scheduled locker clean out, and thought it was inappropriate and questionable enough to run it by Mitch. I was curious about his living circumstances because he had a brief relationship with Susan. I didn't see his Jeep in the parking lot, but went to knock on the apartment door anyway and realized the door was locked. Then I explained that Bob was off work today and how he came to the gym to question me about going to his apartment just as I was closing up. He told me about the neighbor's phone photo of me at his place. I guess he was tired of me nosing around and felt that I knew too much about his involvement in the murders. I really didn't know for sure, just had speculation and suspicion based on the necklace. I repeated the conversation we had, including his confession to both murders, but did not know Mitch was inside until Bob pulled his gun and she yelled for him to stop.

Detective Andrews called and said Bob was claiming innocence. They sent a crime scene unit over to his apartment. At that point Mitch pulled out her phone which had an audio recorder device to replay the conversation. She looked at me. I knew she had been waiting to see how I was going to explain my presence at Bob's apartment. She was willing to stick behind my story, as it was close enough to the truth. Max was holding my hand the whole time. The questioning seemed to take hours, because Mitch and I had to repeat our stories again. I think maybe since I had been a victim of crimes, the police didn't really question if I had committed one or if I had entered his apartment. His confession and attempt on my life made my discovery meaningless, except that seeing the shrine provided information to Mitch and me.

I am befuddled to think that Bob would never have been a suspect and would never have been held accountable for his crimes if he hadn't made a confession when coming after me. I wonder how many crimes turn out that way. No one would have considered trivia Bob as a threat, and he killed two people. Susan and Mick would never have been avenged or exonerated.

FORTY-ONE

I WAS AT home the next day with Max staying right next to me. We took Matt for a walk in the forest preserve. Bundled up in our down jackets, gloves and hats, I needed a little normalcy and nature usually helps. Besides, making Matt happy is so easy, it's contagious!

After lunch, Sam called on my cell phone.

"How are you?" I asked. "I heard the news about Amanda and wondered how you were feeling."

"I'm okay. I also heard your news and wondered how you were feeling."

"I'm okay."

"Well I guess we are both victims of people we cared about. We're both safe and hopefully there will be no more violence."

"Listen, Sam, thank you for all your concern and caring. Thank you for your help with the security and protection. I'm really glad you are healing and will be back to working out soon."

"We can always pick up where we left off, you the trainer, me the client."

"Yeah, we can always do that."

We were both tentative and choosing our words carefully, but feeling a whole lot of crazy emotions. We were caught up in life, not always knowing the answers like most people.

Mitch called next and said that the goons were leaving town because they knew Mick's death wasn't related to the real estate deal. Charles was in pursuit, staying in the background waiting for a chance to catch the big fish.

"When he does solve the case, he said the local newspaper in MidTown would have the story suggesting Mick was a hero for calling in help when he discovered the embezzlement case."

Charlene drove over to the house bringing a variety box of donuts.

"I can't believe it! I just can't believe it! Bob! Trivia Bob! I guess we don't need the séance anymore do we?"

"Probably not, unless you are on some sort of spiritual quest. Do you really want to get involved with the spirits like that?"

"I've always been interested and questioned what the truth is about talking to the dead. I'm not sure I need to know just yet. By the way, are we getting paid while the gym is closed?"

"Yes. I can tell your interest in spirits runs deep, Charlene!"

Marissa and Steve arrived for a family dinner. We decided to go and eat bison burgers and onion rings! As I looked at the four of us, I was happy to be alive and together and thrilled this whole murder episode was behind us. Time to move on and get back to business.

Where do you workout? What is your favorite type of exercise? On a scale of 0 – 10, 0 being a couch potato, and 10 being great, where would you rate your fitness level? Would you like to sign up at OverTheTop to begin the fitness program of your dreams? Have we got a package for you!

ABOUT THE AUTHOR

Combining fitness and fiction, Nancy Klotz is the author this murder mystery, *OverTheTop, A "Dying to Be Fit" Novel*. She is a personal trainer, yoga teacher, group fitness instructor, and health coach in the health and wellness industry. Over the years, she has had several well-loved dogs, and now her children bring their dogs over to visit. She lives in Illinois with her handsome and intriguing husband.